THE TOUCH OF HELL

The village of Shepthorne wasn't being gripped, but strangled by winter's blanket of snow and Arctic temperatures. The trouble began with a massive pile-up on frozen roads and a fireball of exploding petrol as a truck collided with a tanker in the garage forecourt. Then, from the sky, a huge military transport with its cargo of devastation crashed down towards the village. Hell was just beginning to touch Shepthorne . . .

MICHAEL R. LINAKER

THE TOUCH OF HELL

Complete and Unabridged

LINFORD
Leicester

First published in Great Britain

First Linford Edition
published 2007

Copyright © 1981 by Michael R. Linaker
All rights reserved

British Library CIP Data

Linaker, Michael R.
  The touch of hell.—Large print ed.—
Linford mystery library
  1. Disasters—Fiction
  2. Winter storms—Fiction
  3. Suspense fiction
  4. Large type books
  I. Title
  823.9'14 [F]

ISBN 978–1–84617–912–9

Published by
F. A. Thorpe (Publishing)
Anstey, Leicestershire

Set by Words & Graphics Ltd.
Anstey, Leicestershire
Printed and bound in Great Britain by
T. J. International Ltd., Padstow, Cornwall

This book is printed on acid-free paper

Dedicated to the memory of my father —
who will be remembered with
love and affection –– by all of us.

CAUSE

1

The snow had been falling steadily since early the previous evening. It had been a heavy fall, constant throughout the night, and by the early hours of the following morning it lay feet thick on the ground. Even as the grey dawn began to break the temperature dropped, adding freezing conditions to the already bleak weather. Bitter winds swept in from the northeast, pushing the snow into deep, curving drifts. The weight of layered snow began to put stress on the branches of trees, rooftops, even causing telephone cables to sag. With the onset of the freeze, standing vehicles became encased in solid sheets of ice. The contents of radiators and engine-blocks froze, the expanding water bursting rubber hoses and even the cores of metal radiators. Road surfaces, carpeted with snow, turned to deadly strips of ice.

* * *

Traffic began to build up from around 6 a.m. onwards. It was a Monday. The first day of a new working week, and the roads were shortly to be invaded by a stream of both commercial and private vehicles. Driving conditions were hazardous. The roads presented treacherous challenges to the drivers who ventured on to them. Low temperatures caused problems for windscreen wipers and interior heaters. Driving became a test of skill and a trial of patience — both were in short supply.

On the motorway a series of minor accidents created delaying holdups. Drivers were unable to move off again after stopping, wheels spinning on the hard-packed, frozen snow. Others were reluctant to stop in case they found themselves in similar circumstances and tried to weave their way past obstructions. More often than not these tactics caused further stoppages.

Frustrations led to anger — anger to impulsive reactions. Flashing speed-restrictions were ignored as the stream of southbound vehicles rolled on. Speed was increased and maintained.

A blue Marina, travelling in the centre lane, swung out as the driver spotted what he thought was a gap in the fast lane. His windows were badly misted and he failed to see the articulated container lorry moving along the outer lane. The front bumper of the tractor unit smashed into his offside rear wing. Metal buckled. Ripped. The mass of the articulated vehicle drove relentlessly forward. The Marina spun. Out of control. Already beginning to tilt. The nearside front tyre burst under the pressure, allowing the wheel's metal rim to dig into the surface of the motorway. It held just long enough to allow the weight of the lorry to roll it on its side. From there its own bulk did the rest. Dropping over on to its roof the Marina began to drift across the motorway. Trailing a stream of sparks in its wake it ploughed into the mass of vehicles around it. A Volkswagen tried to avoid the hurtling machine — the driver simply jamming on his brakes — and created yet another hazard. The Volkswagen skidded,

5

clipping the rear of a new Jaguar. Within seconds there was a domino effect as vehicle after vehicle became involved.

⋆ ⋆ ⋆

The motorway came to a shuddering, wrenching halt. At the head of the long tailback of vehicles, a mangled, twisted clutch of metal and glass. Of rubber and plastic and human flesh. The grey snow was rainbowed by spilt oil and antifreeze, diesel and petrol. And dappled with the fresh gleam of blood. Stalling engines rattled, then faded into coughing silence.

From the depths of the crushed vehicles a man began to moan. Nearby someone screamed. The sound was high, wavering, and it was difficult to tell whether it issued from man or woman. Yet another, as awareness returned, felt the cruel pain of his terrible injuries. He was trapped in a web of buckled, sheared metal, unable to move. But he was able to see the extent of his wounds. Forced to lie helpless as his lifeblood spurted and pulsed from the mutilated flesh.

6

Somewhere, lost in the remains of a crushed vehicle, a radio played on. The breezy, unceasing flow of words from the disc-jockey, interrupted by the odd record, drifted out over the scene of chaotic devastation.

* * *

Jenny Morrish peered through the misted windscreen, impatience clouding her pretty face. Ahead of her three solid lanes of traffic faded into the silent curtain of falling snow. Jenny took another glance at her watch. She sighed. Might as well relax, she thought. No way you are going to make that appointment now, my girl! The delay had already lasted for over half an hour. The indications pointed to a major accident somewhere up ahead. A really bad one judging by the ambulances, recovery trucks and even a fire appliance, that had sped by on the hard shoulder. And the police cars, sirens wailing and lights flashing.

She leaned forward and craned her neck as she heard the approaching sound of an amplified voice. A police Range Rover appeared, cruising slowly along the hard shoulder. Jenny rolled down her passenger window and listened for a repeat of the message.

'The motorway is completely blocked due to a severe multiple accident. It will be three or four hours before the lanes can be cleared. All traffic is being diverted off the motorway at the Shepthorne exit. If drivers will follow the Shepthorne road they will be able to rejoin the motorway nineteen miles south at Junction 7. The motorway is completely blocked . . . '

As the Range Rover drifted away Jenny closed the window. She turned on the car's ignition. The Triumph TR7 burst into life. Ahead of Jenny the lines of traffic began to move. She let out the clutch and the car edged forward, tyres slipping a little before they achieved a solid grip.

The long streams of cars gained a little speed as they spaced out. Jenny settled back in the padded seat, checking that her safety belt was secured, grateful that at least they were now moving.

* * *

Easing into a higher gear Ron Stanly let the heavy Volvo truck roll easily along the inner lane. He reached for the pack of cigarettes on the wide dash-panel and shook one free. He was in the act of lighting it when he spotted the exit markers coming up. Glancing at his watch he swore out loud. He was already way behind on his schedule and now there was this bloody diversion! God knows where he'd end up! He angrily jerked the lever that operated the flasher-lamps, indicating his change of direction. As the truck rolled on to the exit ramp Ron felt the rear wheels drift. He checked the movement and allowed the Volvo to slow as he caught up with the traffic already on the ramp.

At the bottom of the ramp stood a parked police car. Its flashing roof-lights cast pale bands of orange and red across the snow-covered ground. A police officer, muffled in a thick parka, was directing the traffic on to the road chosen as the diversion route. Ron swung the truck round the curve in the road and reluctantly fell in behind a battered Transit van. He caught a glimpse of a snow-spattered roadsign as he eased on to the narrow road: Shepthorne 15 Miles. He groaned softly. Fifteen bloody miles! At the rate the traffic was moving it was going to take a couple of hours to get there! And then there was the run from the village back to the next motorway junction. He banged his fist on the rim of the steering wheel. It was going to take all sodding day! No guarantee he'd get back either with the way the weather was going! Ron was rapidly beginning to wish he'd listened to Doreen. She'd told him to phone in to say he couldn't make the run because of the weather. Nobody could have argued against that. If he'd taken her advice he would still have been wrapped up in bed with her. She was a great girl — Doreen — a very affectionate girl, and very obliging. A damn sight more fun than being stuck in a line of traffic that was practically stationary, on some unknown little country road, in the middle of a bloody great snowstorm!

Ahead of him, the Transit jerked to a halt. Ron stood on his brakes and felt the truck shudder. The wheels locked and the Volvo began to slide. It came to a stop with less than an inch to spare. Ron's momentary alarm faded and wild anger rose in its place. He hurled a stream of choice obscenities at the unseen driver of the Transit. His abuse was wasted, the expletives fading out of existence in the heated confines of the cab. No one would have taken much notice anyway. The kind word and tolerant thought were in short supply that day.

* * *

Mike Sandler replaced the cap on the Thermos flask and placed it on the floor of the car. He took a quick swallow from the cup in his hand and gasped as scalding coffee burned his lower lip.

'Too hot to handle?' asked the girl in the passenger seat.

Mike grinned at her. 'You know me, Katy,' he said. 'If I get burned I just naturally come back for more.'

The girl glanced up from her notepad. 'Yes — I had noticed.' She leaned across the back of her seat and made a quick adjustment to the radio-transmitter that filled the rear section of the Escort Estate. Slipping a pair of headphones over her thick brown hair she picked up a hand-microphone. 'You still there, Jerry?' She smiled at the reply that came over the headphones. 'Well put it away, love, and switch on your little recorder. Ready? We're about a mile outside Shepthorne now. No sign of the weather improving at all. Snow still falling very heavily. The road is only just passable. Traffic's bumper to bumper. Police are having a hell of a job keeping it moving. I'll try and get a piece talking to one of the top-brass if any of them are around and we can use it on the mid-morning spot. Use what I've just given you for the next local news item. If I can set it up in time John can bring me in live for an update on conditions round about ten-thirty. All right, Jerry? What? It's really lousy out here! Listen, we're going to drive on now, and see if we can get into Shepthorne.

Talk to you then.'

Mike passed a cup of coffee over as Kathy Young removed the headphones. She took it gratefully and stared out through the streaked windscreen.

'Think we can get through?' she asked.

Mike's answer was to start the car, slip into gear, and swing the Escort off the side of the road in a spray of churned-up snow. Oblivious to the flashing headlights and the blaring horns, he took the car along the right-hand side of the road. Kathy clung to her cup of coffee in sheer desperation.

'I suppose it serves me right for asking,' she muttered to herself.

Mike somehow managed to avoid the deep, frozen ruts covering the surface of the road, and Kathy had to acknowledge his driving skill.

'If this snow keeps on coming,' she said, 'we're going to find ourselves stranded.'

'You mean just the two of us and the radio?' Mike grinned. 'Now that could be interesting.'

'Don't let your imagination run away with you, lover.'

'It's a situation just full of romance,' Mike pointed out. 'Handsome man. Nubile, beautiful girl. Trapped together in a confined space. Intimate closeness forced on them in the interests of survival. Their bounding passions matching the natural fury of the raging storm.'

'My God, I wish I'd got that on tape!' Kathy shook her head, laughing. 'With lines like that you could be the Barbara Cartland of radio.'

'Gee, Miss Young,' he drawled in a nasal American accent, 'do you really and truly mean that?'

'Shut up, you idiot, and just concentrate on the road.'

Ahead of them the narrow road began to curve off to the left. Out of the swirling snow-mist the humped outlines of houses began to emerge. Mike steered the Escort around a truck and then they were entering Shepthorne.

Kathy leaned forward, pointing along the village's single street. 'Patrol car there,' she said. 'Pull up behind it and I'll see if we can pick up some news.'

A uniformed figure trudged towards them as Mike braked the radio-car. Kathy rolled down her window, nodding to the police officer.

'Hello, then,' the officer said, leaning in at the window. 'You lost, miss?'

'Sergeant Roderick,' Kathy smiled. 'My favourite policeman.'

'A little respect, young woman,' Roderick said. He nodded at Mike. 'What's it like back there?'

'Traffic's backed up for miles,' Mike told him. 'And it's still coming off the motorway.'

Roderick sighed. 'Why can't the silly buggers stay at home on a day like this!'

'Can I use that word for word?' Kathy asked.

'You do and we'll both be out of a job!'

'Well, how about doing a little piece for the next situation update?' Kathy asked. 'Give them one of your cautionary monologues.'

'Cheeky.' Roderick wagged a finger at Kathy. 'One day I'm going to find a nice quiet little cell for you.'

15

'Lucky you,' Mike lisped. 'He's never made me a proposition like that.'

'Sergeant? What about the chat?'

'I suppose so,' Roderick said.

Kathy dragged out a heavy portable tape-recorder. She pulled the hood of her parka up and climbed out of the car.

'Mike,' she called. 'Link up with Jerry and see how much tape-time he wants.'

It was exactly 9.23 when he began to speak to the studio.

* * *

'Bloody hell!'

The harsh voice penetrated Dawn Stanton's soporific state. She willed one eye to open and peered out over the edge of the bedclothes. As her hazy vision cleared she made out Sam Mayhew's broad-shouldered, muscular figure planted solidly in front of the hotel room's window. He had yanked back the curtains and was bracing himself against the window-frame, his big hands gripping the wood tightly.

'Sam?' Dawn opened her other eye. 'What's the matter?'

'Go back to sleep,' he snapped, his tone implying there was nothing else to talk about.

Dawn rolled over, curling her naked body into a warm ball. She pulled the bedclothes up over her chin. There was no sense in trying to talk with Sam if he was in one of his moods. There were times, Dawn decided, when Sam Mayhew was a real pain in the arse! Which was a shame. Because he could be really nice. Fun to be with, and great in bed. Dawn wriggled her hips, a soft fluttering rising in her stomach. Damn you, Sam, I could just fancy you right now! She pouted — there wasn't much chance of that now! Not with him turning all miserable! Dawn sighed. If she wanted anything this morning she was going to have to play solo. Well she could do that too! And serve him right! She let the fingers of her right hand stray between her firm thighs . . .

'Just my bloody luck!' Sam's voice crackled from the other side of the room.

Dawn allowed herself a silent curse as

she pushed the bedclothes aside and sat up.

'For heaven's sake, Sam, what is the matter?' she demanded.

Sam Mayhew turned from the window and scowled at the young, redhaired girl sitting up in the middle of the bed. The fact that she was naked did nothing to soothe his sullen mood.

'Take a bloody look outside!' he snarled and stalked off to the bathroom, slamming the door behind him.

Kicking aside the bedclothes Dawn slid off the bed and padded to the window. Her face formed into a pleased smile as she saw the snow outside. She stood watching it, and the line of slow-moving vehicles fumbling their way along the narrow road running through the village.

'I don't see why you're making all that fuss,' she called. 'It's only a bit of snow.'

The bathroom door swung open and Sam came out.

'I'm supposed to be attending a meeting of the directors this afternoon — that's why I'm making a fuss!'

'Don't you ever forget about that damn bank?'

Sam finished buttoning his shirt and snatched up his tie. 'If it wasn't for the bank and the high salary it pays me, we wouldn't be able to enjoy these little jaunts!' Knotting the tie with sharp, impatient movements Sam crossed to the dressing table. He began to pick up his personal belongings and slip them in his pockets. 'If you want any breakfast you'd better get some bloody clothes on!'

'You have such an elegant way of expressing things, Sammy dear.'

Dawn began to wander around the room, searching for the clothes she'd deposited in various places the night before.

'Dawn, get a move on. As soon as we've had breakfast I want to . . . '

Pulling on her skirt she threw him an angry look. 'Don't worry, Sam, *I* wouldn't want to be the one to keep you from your beloved, bloody bank!' She glanced at her watch, wondering what all the fuss was about — after all it was only 9.23.

19

Major Vivian Dolby, retired, had woken that morning with a feeling of uncharacteristic loneliness. Dolby was a self-sufficient, contented man. True, he was set in his ways — even somewhat on the anachronistic side. He would have admitted to both criticisms. He went his own way, holding on to a set of values far above those of the present day. Yet that was no crime. He intruded on no one, nor did his existence interfere with anyone else. He allowed the hectic pace of life to pass him by, and within the boundaries of his world Dolby had found a containable level of satisfaction.

Yet loneliness had somehow infiltrated his domain . . .

He had woken as usual at 8 o'clock, and had lain there staring at the shadowed ceiling of his bedroom. Normally he rose quickly and would be in the kitchen making a pot of tea within a few minutes of waking. But not this day; he lay and he gazed at the ceiling and he tried to work out in his mind just what lay ahead of him.

He was fifty-five years old, unmarried and with few friends. His closest companions had been the men he had served with in the army. When he had left, promises had been made all round about maintaining contact. Everyone was so determined to keep their word. But the days and weeks passed. Months. Then years. What little communication remained slowly drifted away. Soon all Dolby had left was the small gunshop he'd opened in '71. Business had never been more than tolerable, yet Dolby made a living. Coupled with his army pension it added up to a reasonable enough income. Dolby was a good housekeeper. He was cautious, spent wisely, and never overindulged. He had his books, his record collection. He enjoyed painting watercolours, and time slid by pleasantly.

And that was when he woke one morning and asked himself just what the hell was he doing with his life? It was only when he tried to answer that he suddenly realised just how empty and friendless his life was. In the same fraction of a second he knew, too, that being aware of the situation did nothing to provide a satisfactory solution. There was no instant cure for loneliness. No incantation that would conjure up a circle of friends to fill the void. There was an overwhelming surge of inner rage — against the unknown cause of his present feelings. He couldn't understand why he was suddenly being stricken by this sensation of emptiness. Was it merely a long-suppressed need for companionship? Or an awareness of how many lost years lay behind him?

Dolby sat up suddenly. He realised he had been slipping into a half-sleep, his mind drifting. He climbed stiffly out of bed and crossed the bedroom. Opening the curtains he stared out on a scene of utter chaos. Thick snow covered the ground. More was driving down out of a heavy, grey sky. The village's single road was solid with slow-moving vehicles. Dolby glanced at his watch. Was that really the time? He was going to lose half the morning if he didn't get a move on!

That was a state he was going to have to change — there had been too much time wasted in the past. Shivering slightly against the room's chill air he dressed hurriedly and went to the bathroom. A few minutes later he was on his way downstairs.

It was 9.23.

★   ★   ★

Hunching his shoulders beneath the thick sheepskin coat Harrison Bryant trudged slowly through the thick snow covering the grass verge running parallel with the River Shep. The river ran through the village, curving away at the eastern edge where it flowed under the old stone bridge that carried the road out of the village.

The tall, blond young American was oblivious to the heavy snowfall. He was far removed from reality, for as he walked his mind was creating and rejecting ideas with frightening regularity. The trouble was that none of the ideas were what he was looking for. Reluctantly Harrison was coming close to admitting that his stay in Shepthorne hadn't worked out.

Harrison Bryant had lost himself in Shepthorne's peaceful atmosphere so that he could hopefully complete his latest book. For weeks now he'd been struggling with a section of the manuscript dealing with events vital to the main theme of the novel. Up to now he'd been unsuccessful. He was working on the fourth rewrite of the section, and even before completing it he knew he still hadn't got it right. His publisher was starting to fret because a deadline was fast approaching, and it was already an extended deadline. Harrison had talked him into a further two weeks. He wanted desperately to get the script completed. But he knew now that he wasn't going to do it here in Shepthorne.

The traditional, old English village atmosphere had offered him the perfect setting. A haven of contemplation. A sanctuary where he could work undisturbed. A friend of Harrison's owned a small cottage on the edge of the village — which he hardly ever used. When he'd heard about Harrison's problem he'd offered the use of the place. Harrison had accepted the offer gratefully — though now he knew he'd made a mistake. Isolation in large doses could be a drawback. The peace and quiet, coupled with the natural reserve of the villagers themselves, had created an almost monastic atmosphere, and Harrison found he was becoming bored. There was no stimulation for his mind in any form — his creative processes were becoming dulled.

Even as he walked slowly along the riverside he made a conscious decision to return to London immediately. Yet that posed a problem in itself.

Harrison paused to survey the unending stream of traffic passing slowly through the village. Cars and lorries drifting in from the top end of the road, looming out of the falling snow, blurred headlights creating rings of hazy illumination. A thin smile touched his lips. He'd wanted something to relieve the boredom. Now he had it. If the snow continued, though, he would find himself marooned in Shepthorne. He wondered how long the traffic was going to block the road. At the rate it was moving it could be all day. Which effectively upset his desire to quit the village. But there was still time for it to slacken off. It was comparatively early yet. Harrison pulled back his sleeve and glanced at his watch.

It read 9.23.

★   ★   ★

'More tea, dear?' Elouise Smythe asked across the breakfast table.

Her sister, Allison, looked up from the pages of the book she was reading. 'Have we time?'

'Plenty of time, dear. I don't really think there's much point in opening the shop today. I can't see many people coming out in this weather.'

'But we always open the shop, Elouise.' Allison pushed aside her book. 'I just wouldn't feel right if we didn't open.'

'If it will make you happier, dear, then of course we will open.'

Allison smiled, relieved. 'I don't know

what I'd do if you weren't here.'

'Don't underestimate yourself.' Elouise stood up. She took the empty breakfast plates to the sink, placing them in hot, soapy water. As she washed the plates she found herself staring out of the kitchen window. The tiny garden at the rear of the house looked so different now that it was covered by a thick blanket of snow. Elouise hated snow. In fact she disliked any kind of cold weather. She longed for the warmth of the sun. Blue skies. Sparkling water sending foamy waves up on a white sandy beach. She smiled wistfully. Soapy water in a sink of dirty dishes was more her style now, she thought. But it hadn't always been that way. Old memories, pushed out of the dusty corners of her mind, refused to retreat, and she found herself reliving a summer back in 1956 . . .

. . . the big white villa overlooking the sun-drenched rooftops of Nice. It was an idyllic life for Elouise and Allison. Elouise had been twenty-two, her sister twenty. Their indulgent father, since the death of their mother five years previously, had given them anything they asked for, allowing them a degree of freedom ahead of its time. It wasn't as if he couldn't afford to be generous. Henry Smythe owned a company that made expensive, custom-built cars that sold all over the world. Elouise and Allison lived off that success — and lived very well. The thought that one day something might happen to change their way of life never entered their pretty heads. So when the bubble did burst Elouise and Allison found themselves suddenly isolated and more than a little lost. They were forced to make a rapid change of lifestyle. From endless luxury to plain and simple survival.

It happened without warning. Their father received a telegram from London. Henry Smythe had made some bad investments. He had also ploughed a great deal of his money into developing a revolutionary new engine. The investments hit rock-bottom and a flaw in the basic design of the new engine meant that without further high funding the project would have to be cancelled. There was a lot of legal wrangling, many desperate, last-minute attempts to come up with a sound solution, but eventually the matter was narrowed down to a simple edict: there was no more money. Within a few weeks the firm went into liquidation and Elouise and Allison saw their way of life vanish for ever. Fortunately their father had been wise enough to provide for such a time. He had placed in trust for his daughters enough money to purchase a small business. The whole matter had been handled by Henry Smythe's solicitor. He had found a dress shop, with living accommodation, in a village, some forty miles from London. A village called Shepthorne. It was typically rural. A community where the old values still meant something, where Elouise and Allison would not feel out of place. The sisters had arrived in Shepthorne in 1957 — and had been there ever since. Their father had disappeared shortly after their arrival. They had a much-travelled postcard from Australia two years later in which their father implied that he was on the verge of setting up a new business venture. There was no mention of what the business was or whether it was likely to succeed. They never heard from their father again.

Now in their mid-forties the sisters were as much a part of Shepthorne as the War Memorial that stood on the Green in the centre of the village. Elouise and Allison. The genteel spinsters, as they were affectionately known. Not that Elouise had always been so easily labelled. Back in the heady days when they had lived in the South of France her time had been taken up by fast cars and handsome young men. She had built a reputation for sharing her favours that had been hard to match. And in 1956 — before her father lost his business and his fortune — Elouise lost something that was most decidely irreplaceable. Her virginity. She gave it willingly to a good-looking young Englishman she'd met during a night-long party on board a private yacht belonging to some million-aire from the Greek islands. While the party went on above decks, Elouise and her partner found themselves a secluded cabin, and there, in the night-warmed shadows they had sprawled naked together on cool silk sheets, bodies thrust together, fingers seeking, touching, exploring . . .

'Shall I go and unlock the shop?'

Elouise returned to reality with a jerk. The plate in her hand slid back into the bowl with a splash.

'Elouise?'

A guilty expression on her flushed face, Elouise glanced over her shoulder.

'Yes, you go and open the shop, dear. I'll be through just as soon as I finish in here.'

Allison smiled. Being allowed to open the shop on her own still gave her a feeling of great responsibility.

As her sister left the kichen Elouise turned her attention to the washing-up. Try as she might she found she was unable to concentrate on the task. Damn! It was thinking about that night in '56 again. And that young man . . . now what was his name? She smiled at her reflection in the kitchen window. My God, she thought, things are coming to a state when you can't even remember the name of the man who deflowered you! Still, she did have the memory of that night. Of how it had felt. Her recall of the event was vivid and often very strong. Especially at night. Alone. In bed. Elouise felt her colour rise again. No, damn it, she protested. I won't let it embarrass me! My own thoughts are just that — mine! They can't offend anyone and they don't offend me. Why shouldn't I have my own personal little fantasy? By present day standards what she'd done all those years back was barely worth mentioning. It wasn't as if she'd spent her life sleeping with man after man. Her sexual encounters over the years had been moderate — but satisfying to a degree. Elouise sighed, and pulled her thoughts back to more mundane affairs. She stared down at the bowl of dishes, at her hands red from the hot water. Come on, my girl, get your mind out of the bedroom and back in the . . .

'Elouise!'

Allison's voice interrupted her concentration. She glanced over her shoulder, saw her sister framed in the doorway.

'Do you realise what time it is? We've never been so late opening the shop.' Allison tapped the face of her wristwatch. 'It's almost 9.30!'

United States Air Force Base,
Milwich, England

'Skybird 104 to Milwich Control! Skybird 104 to Milwich Control! Do you read me, Milwich?'

'Milwich Control to Skybird 104. I'm picking you up again. But you're faint.'

' . . . got a problem, Milwich, and we need you to talk us down!'

'Skybird, what's the trouble?'

' . . . malfunction . . . checking it out . . . electrical . . . '

'I can't read you, Skybird. Skybird, come in. If you can hear *me* try switching to another frequency. Call in Skybird! Call in . . . '

Communications Technician Don Weaver stared at the dull glow coming from the screen of the tracking scanner and watched the green blip that was Skybird 104 drift steadily off course. His eyes flicked from the scanner to the bank of electronic registers, his trained mind deciphering the machine language and translating it into cold facts and figures. He reached for a telephone, punching out an on-base number.

'Major Devine? Weaver, sir, from ComCon. I think you should get down here, Major. We've got problems with your Skybird 104 flight.'

'What kind of problems?'

'Communications contact breaking down, and they appear to be having some internal malfunction.'

'I'll be right down, Weaver. See if you can make contact with them again.'

'Sir.' Weaver put down the phone. He sat staring at the scanner for a moment. Then he activated his headset. 'Milwich Control here. Come in Skybird 104. Do you read me, Skybird?'

There was no response. The receiving loudspeaker emitted only a faint hiss. Weaver ran his pickup through the frequency bands — even the emergency wavelengths. Nothing. He checked his scanner again. Skybird was still there, though well off course now, and starting to lose height.

Major Devine entered the ComCon room, striding briskly across to Weaver's section. Devine, in his early forties, was a service-career man. He'd joined the airforce the moment he became eligible. His natural ability for command had ensured a steady, but moderate promotion. Devine had done tours of duty in Germany and Vietnam. Then a couple of years at Vandenberg before being assigned to duty at Milwich. The service was Devine's life and he took his responsibility as a personal matter. His expression, as he crossed over to Weaver, was an indication of his concern over the man's call.

'You in touch again?' he asked.

Weaver shook his head. 'I can't raise them, sir. I've been right through the frequency bands. Everything. They just don't acknowledge.'

Devine thought for a moment. 'Do you still have visual contact?'

'There they are,' Weaver said. 'Moving way off course now.'

'Damn!' Devine stared hard at the green speck on the screen. 'Did they give you *any* kind of information about their problem?'

'Nothing much, Major,' Weaver said. 'It was about that time the communications went dead. Only thing I got was something about electrical malfunction.'

Leaning forward Devine read the information breakdowns offered by the tracking equipment. Weaver caught the expression on the major's face, and began to wonder just what was so special about Skybird 104. Devine had been fussing about like some paranoid mother hen from the moment they'd been told about the flight arriving. All Weaver knew about it was that it was a Lockheed C–130 Hercules Transport coming in from some Stateside Airforce base in the Midwest. He'd figured out that it must be something pretty important the way Devine was hopping about.

'If she keeps on that course, Weaver — what's your opinion?'

'Hell, major, the way she's losing height, she'll crash!'

Devine banged his fist down on the edge of Weaver's seat. 'Goddamnit!' he snapped. 'All this fancy equipment and we can't do a thing to help one of our own planes!'

Weaver didn't respond. He was focusing his full attention on the scanner, eyes constantly checking and rechecking the information readouts.

'Jesus H Christ!' he exclaimed. 'That son of a bitch must be chopping off treetops!'

'Try and make contact . . . ' Devine snapped.

'Major, if I could talk to Skybird right now I wouldn't be sitting here sweatin' my ass off!'

The remark went unnoticed by Devine. He was gazing, almost hypnotically, at the drifting green dot that was Skybird 104. He shifted his gaze a fraction, reading off the statistical numerations displayed on the panel in front of him. Fine beads of sweat peppered his taut features as he watched in total helplessness — a mute witness to the approaching death of an aircraft and its crew.

On the scanner the green dot stopped moving — and then vanished. The digital readouts registered negative response.

Weaver dragged his eyes from the glowing screen. 'Ground zero, Major.'

Devine swore. 'Weaver, I want that aircraft pinpointed to the last half-inch! And I want it done damn quick! I'll be in my office.'

Weaver nodded absently. He wasn't even aware of Devine's departure. He hunched over his instrument panels, starting to work out the cross-references that would give him the location of the downed aircraft. He took a look at the wall-clock so he could log the time of the crash . . .

9.26.

★　★　★

Devine was breathing hard by the time he reached his office; have to think seriously about some kind of fitness training. The intrusion broke his concentration and he stood hesitatingly by his desk until his mind cleared itself of trivia. Then he picked up the phone and put in his call.

'Major Devine,' he announced when the call was connected with Washington. There was a minimal delay — then the soft pulse of sound told him that the scrambler had been cut in.

'Devine?'

'Mr Conrad, we have a problem.'

There was the slightest hesitation. 'Is it to do with Skybird?'

'I'm afraid so, sir. Skybird has just made some kind of a crash-landing.'

'What's the extent of the damage?'

'At this time we're still pinpointing the exact location of the crash. Skybird was way off course.'

'How did it happen?'

'That's something we can only guess at. All we got was a call about some inflight malfunction and then there was a communications failure. We tracked Skybird to ground zero. I've got my people working out the coordinates now.'

'All right, Major Devine, this is what I want you to do. I want a full security blanket over this. Understood?'

Devine understood enough to know

39

not to ask questions. Whatever, or whoever, had been on that plane appeared to
be important enough to create more than
a little concern.

'I'm going to ring off now,' Conrad
said. 'You'll get a call in a while from
London. A man named Thompson. Give
him your full cooperation, Devine. Tell
him anything he needs to know, and act
on anything he tells you.'

'Yes, sir.'

'In the meantime get the position of
that plane . . . '

The line went dead as Conrad dropped
his receiver. Devine put down his own
phone, reached over to replace it with an
internal one.

'Weaver?'

'That you, Major Devine? I was about
to give you a call, sir. I've got the
coordinates.'

'So where is the damn thing?'

'I double-checked to be sure, Major,'
Weaver said — his tone was almost
apologetic. 'According to the map,
Skybird's come down right on top of a
village. Some place called Shepthorne.'

'Jesus!' Devine muttered.

'Sir?'

'Nothing, Weaver. Just stay available.'

Devine replaced the phone. He sat down behind his desk and stared out of the window. Thin drifts of light snow misted the airfield. Delicate flakes clung to the wet glass of the window, melting slowly and sliding to the bottom of the pane.

* * *

Reg Buck stared sullenly out of the office window at the swirling white flurries of snow rolling across the garage forecourt. He sank his wide shoulders deeper into his thick coat, wondering why he'd bothered to open up. He glanced at his watch. 9.15. None of his staff had turned in and he didn't really blame them. He should have done the same and stayed at home.

Beyond the deserted forecourt lay the road that ran through Shepthorne. A steady stream of traffic had been lurching along the road since before 8. Reg had picked up the report of the motorway accident on the radio. He allowed himself a wry smile as he watched the line of traffic. He could have done with traffic like this during the long summer months. The motorway had deprived the village of a fair amount of trade. On the other hand it had improved the quality of life. Shepthorne had returned to its former state of tranquillity and Reg had to admit it was pleasant.

The sound of a truck horn caught his attention. Reg turned to look out through the office window. A long petrol tanker was crawling slowly across the forecourt, to one side of the three snow-shrouded pumps. Reg buttoned up his coat and turned up his collar. He jammed on an old hat, pulled gloves over his hands. Jerking open the door he stepped into the slashing blast of snow. His booted feet sank in the curving drifts banked up near the door.

A hooded figure was climbing down out of the cab as Reg reached the tanker.

'You pick your days!' Reg said.

The tanker driver grinned from the

depths of his parka-hood. 'I can take it back if you don't want it.'

'No bloody chance,' Reg said. He scraped snow away from the iron cover over the storage tank intake pipes. 'What have you brought?'

'Fifteen-hundred of 4 star and the same of 3.' The driver climbed up on to the top of the tanker and slid dipsticks into the tanks. He showed the sticks to Reg who checked the levels and nodded. Down on the ground again the driver coupled up the feed-pipe to the first storage tank, started his engine and opened the valve. Petrol began to flow through the pipe.

'You making any more calls?' Reg asked.

The driver shook his head. 'You're the first and last today. I didn't reckon on it getting as bad as this.'

'You fancy a cup of tea?'

'Yeah.'

'I'll put the kettle on.' Reg turned and trudged back towards the office.

He was reaching out to push open the office door when he heard a pulsing roar of sound. For a moment he couldn't place where it was coming from. It seemed to be everywhere. All around him and growing louder with each second. Reg glanced over his shoulder, and in that moment the tanker driver gave a yell, his words lost in the throbbing swell of noise. He was pointing skywards. Reg raised his eyes. A huge dark shape drifted down out of the heavy, snow-filled sky. It swept in over the low roof of the cottage standing just beyond the garage, its gigantic bulk blotting out the light. The roar of noise increased, beating against Reg's ears, and he realised what it was in a fleeting, final moment of awareness.

A huge aircraft!

And then he thought — *my God, it's coming down on the village!*

* * *

The road curved round to the left as it entered the village. Ron Stanly hauled on the Volvo's wheel, felt the tyres grip the hard-packed snow. He'd decided to stop once he reached the village. Park

44

somewhere and find a place where he could get a drink and maybe a late breakfast. As he rolled around the bend he saw the lights of a petrol station on the opposite side of the road. A petrol tanker was pulled in near the pumps. Ron had a quick look at his fuel; the tank was well over half full.

Above the sound of the Volvo's engine he picked up a deeper, heavier roar. Something attracted his attention; a darkness in the sky; looming and expanding. Ron jerked his head round.

'Christ!'

The single word was lost in the abrupt roar of noise that filled the Volvo's cab. Ron jammed his foot hard down on the throttle pedal, ignoring the fact that the road was iced over beneath the thick snow. All he could think of was getting out of the way of the monstrous thing dropping out of the sky — coming down towards him at frightening speed.

He knew he wasn't going to make it. That the thing was going to hit him. But the possibility that he might die never crossed his mind. Like most individuals in a moment of extreme crisis he acted without concern for the ultimate risk. It was pure survival instinct. In Ron Stanly's case it was a useless gesture.

There was a solid thump at the rear of the truck. Ron felt it begin to slide across the road, propelled by some invisible force. He went through the motions of steering, braking, while his eyes remained firmly fixed on the scene before him.

The front wheels of the truck bounced over the low wall fronting the garage forecourt, then rolled on, smashing heavily into the rear of the parked petrol tanker.

Ron Stanly felt himself lifted from his seat. He tried to hang on to the steering wheel, but the force of the impact overcame his frail strength. He was hurled through the already disintegrating windscreen, his body slamming up against the rear of the tanker. Pain flared briefly, then drifted away into total darkness. He was not aware of the way in which his shattered body was crushed, flesh mangled by sheared metal.

★ ★ ★

The impact of the truck hitting the rear of the tanker split the seams of the rear section. Petrol flooded from the gaps. The tanker itself was shoved forward a couple of yards, tearing free the feed-pipe connecting it to the storage tank. Petrol, still being pumped out under pressure, gushed across the forecourt.

The crippled truck's rear swung round on the slippery surface of the forecourt, ripping the three pumps off their concrete bases.

Reg Buck stood and watched the inevitable take place. Even though his brain reacted to the situation, registering the extreme danger, his body failed to respond swiftly enough. He knew he should at least try to seek safety — even while he was realising he had no time left.

Shattered sections of the petrol pumps filled the air. The stricken truck began to topple slowly over on to its side. In the periphery of his vision Reg could still see the pale stream of petrol gushing from the severed feed-pipe, more bubbling from the rear of the tanker.

A severed electric cable from one of the pumps drooped to the ground. The exposed inner wiring brushed against a twisted metal section, all that remained of one of the pumps. An arcing crackle of sparks showered across the forecourt . . . petrol flared in an instant, spreading out and up, swelling with terrifying speed. The forecourt became a mass of searing flame. Rippling tongues raced out across the concrete — reaching, searching, leaping up the side of the tanker and homing in on the fractured seams at the rear of the vehicle. There was a solid thump, rising to a sucking, demonic roar, and then the tanker vanished in a huge ball of flame as its contents ignited, the pressure ripping open the confining vessel. The underground storage tanks erupted with a shattering explosion. Shock waves flattened the front wall of the garage and somewhere in amongst the debris lay the lacerated bodies of Reg Buck and the tanker driver. Hundreds of gallons of petrol became an instant fireball that took on a deliberate force of its own. It swept across the garage forecourt and reached out along the snow-covered street, the brilliant glare of flame illuminating the destruction in the wake of the hurtling juggernaut that had descended on the hapless village.

★   ★   ★

Skybird 104 literally sheared off rooftops, sending tons of debris crashing down through the interiors of buildings. Early in its sweep over the village one of the huge engines was torn from the port wing. The stricken aircraft drifted off towards the left side of the street. A wingtip touched the ground, disintegrating — but not before the aircraft demolished the remaining buildings at the far end of the street. Becoming suddenly dead weight as its velocity faded, the giant Hercules hit the ground, clawing deep furrows out of the very earth. It slithered in a destructive quarter-circle before it came to a wrenching halt, tail up, the foresection of the huge fuselage coming to rest on the stone bridge that allowed access to or exit from the village by carrying the road over the River Shep.

⋆   ⋆   ⋆

Jenny Morrish had been midway through the village when the explosion at the garage filled the sky with a blinding light. She took a terrified glance in her rearview mirror and saw the boiling mass of howling flame leaping along the street towards her. She wrenched the wheel of the car to the left, taking it up on to the grass verge. A gentle slope lay before her and beyond the gleam of water — the River Shep.

She sensed a moving shape on the left of her car. It was a heavy lorry, the rear section billowing with orange flame. Jenny knew it was going to hit her. She hugged the steering wheel. A second later she felt the impact. The force of the contact spun the lighter car round, and for a heart-wrenching moment Jenny was certain the TR7 would roll over. Then the nearside wheels settled against the ground again and the car slithered the rest of the way down the slope to the river's edge. The front wheels dropped and a silver sheen of water cascaded over the windscreen. The TR7 slid forward, the bonnet sinking beneath the surface. For a moment it balanced on the edge of the crumbling bank. Jenny sat motionless. She hardly dared to breathe. Abruptly the TR7 jerked forward again, tilting, the rear coming up off the ground. Jenny watched in silent horror as water bubbled up over the rear of the bonnet and reached the base of the wind-screen. It began to trickle into the footwell, dripping down on her legs from beneath the dash. She gasped as the ice-cold water soaked through her trousers. The shock of the water on her flesh snapped her out of her daze. She had to get out of the car. She dropped her left hand and pressed the release on the seatbelt. As the belt opened Jenny worked the interior handle on the door. It refused to budge. She jerked at it — part in anger, part in fear. The door remained tightly shut. Jenny glanced down and saw that the inner frame of the door was buckled inwards. The impact of the lorry against the car had pushed the whole body out of shape, jamming the door tight.

'Damn!' Jenny leaned across and tried to open the other door. It was stuck as well. She considered for a moment. Perhaps she could kick one of the doors open! She made to swing her legs up across the seats, and found that her left ankle was caught between the clutch and the bulkhead where the engine protruded into the passenger compartment. Forgetting about the doors for a moment Jenny tried to free her ankle; she only managed to cause an unexpected burst of pain that speared up her leg. Cold sweat beaded her face as she flopped back against the seat in agony.

It was only as the pain began to slowly subside that she became aware of a slow, but steady forward movement as the TR7 settled, little by little, into the cold water of the river . . .

★ ★ ★

Rolling sheets of flame fanned out across the road, melting the fallen snow, then licking at the bodywork of slow-moving cars and trucks. Superheated paint blistered and blackened, windows and windscreens shattered. Startled drivers found themselves enveloped in scorching heat that sucked the very moisture from their bodies. Clothing burst into flame, flesh shrivelled from bone under the terrible heat. Car interiors were turned into flaming traps where writhing forms made frantic — though brief — efforts to escape; few did; they died in the first blast of flame and were left black and shrunken, melted into the softened plastic of car seats. Along the line of vehicles fuel tanks began to explode, each adding its fire and fury to the scene; they ignited with dull, solid sounds, sending blazing fuel skywards. Out of this boiling sea of flame staggered a burning figure. Flames devoured living flesh even as the shrieking caricature of a man lurched and stumbled and danced in a grisly pantomime of horror before shrinking to the ground. More fuel tanks exploded as the hungry flames dashed along the line of vehicles. Drivers seeing what was coming scattered from their vehicles, running, throwing themselves to the ground. Some escaped. Others were not so lucky and were caught by the secondary explosions as more and more lethal fuel ignited.

★   ★   ★

The first indication of something being wrong manifested itself as a rapidly increasing vibration that filled Vivian Dolby's kitchen. He had only entered a minute or so earlier, crossing the room to fill the kettle. Crockery, on a wall-shelf, began to tremble. Dolby raised his head and stared at the pottery. He turned off the tap and put down the kettle as the vibration deepened He could hear a muted sound now — a droning, rhythmic effect that got louder and louder.

Dolby walked out of the kitchen. He paused at the bottom of the stairs, frowning at the sound as it rose with frightening speed; it seemed to pulsate from the very walls. He took a step forward . . . hesitant . . .

The house shook beneath the noise. The floor moved under Dolby's feet. Jagged cracks disfigured the plaster ceiling of the hallway. Pale dust shimmered from the cracks. The noise was deafening now, tearing at his senses. It made his head throb. His eyes ached.

Walls began to collapse around him. Somewhere in the house glass shattered. Part of the ceiling crashed down into the hall. Choking dust billowed around Dolby's motionless figure. He began to cough. The dust was fine and acrid. At the top of the stairs the bedroom door flew off its hinges as falling masonry smashed it free. Dolby stared in stunned amazement as he realised that he could see the sky through what had once been the bedroom ceiling.

He jerked into movement. The door! He had to reach the door! Get outside before . . . A solid object struck him across the back of his skull. Dolby gasped in pain, falling forward against the wall. His legs gave way and he slumped to the floor. Debris showered down on him.

Dolby clawed at the wall. He could feel blood streaming down the back of his neck. A cold sickness rose in his stomach. He must get out! Before the whole house came down on him! He knew it was what he had to do — he wasn't certain whether he could manage it.

★ ★ ★

The inner port engine, torn from the shattered wing, was projected forward on a separate trajectory from the aircraft itself. Despite its dead weight the engine contained enough velocity to carry it over three buildings before it dropped down through the roof of the Shepthorne Arms Hotel . . .

Solid oak and hand-hewn stone that had stood up to the impact of two hundred years of elemental fury yielded under the destructive impact of hurtling metal. Through attic initially, splintering main support beams, tearing free electric cables and water pipes, where the gathered dust of decades was showered on to the floor below along with cascading debris. A rending crack rose amid the general din as the weakened floor sagged, then caved in beneath the overwhelming weight. Windows shattered with the resultant impact, glass exploding out into the road, and then thick clouds of dust spewed up from the shattered building.

★   ★   ★

Sam Mayhew was partway through the door when the ceiling caved in. He heard the splintering crash of wood, the rattling patter of falling plaster. He turned, alarmed by the violent eruption of noise. A heavy roar filled the air. The building began to shudder. A fine mist of pale dust stung his face. Then something smashed down across the back of Sam's shoulders. Against his will he was driven forward, the unknown weight pressing him down, crushing him to the floor. Sam braced his hands flat against the carpet and attempted to push himself upright again but the oppressive weight over-whelmed him. As he lay there he heard

Dawn's voice, almost childlike, calling for him.

★ ★ ★

An invisible hand threw Elouise Smythe across the kitchen. She struck the edge of the doorframe, catching her left cheek on the sharp angle. Pain flared instantly, strong enough to make her cry out. She clutched her hands to her face, and felt blood pulse out from between her fingers.

Behind her the kitchen seemed to be falling apart. Debris rained down from the ruined ceiling, filling the air with dust. The far wall suddenly crumbled and a large section of the ceiling fell in and buried the sink.

Elouise climbed slowly to her feet and stumbled away from the door.

'Elouise!'

'Where are you?'

Allison's thin voice drifted out of the dusty shadows. 'Please help me, Elouise! It does hurt so very much!'

★ ★ ★

Harrison Bryant was a witness to the initial destruction visited upon Shepthorne. Disbelief clouded his features as he caught his first glimpse of the gigantic aircraft swooping in on the village at treetop level. He saw a wingtip dip and brush the rear of a truck just entering the village . . .

He felt guilty — almost like some reluctant voyeur — as he watched and found he was able to plot out the pattern of movements in the grim choreography of destruction.

First the truck — swerving in across the garage forecourt — hitting the rear of the tanker delivering petrol — overhead the dark configuration of the aircraft drifting ever lower across the rooftops — touching — ripping brick and stone free — the air filling with flying debris — the aircraft blocking out the daylight as it sank belly-down over the buildings at the far end of the street — and within those scant and frozen seconds the blistering fury of exploding petrol stretching skywards — outwards — the shimmering fireball bursting down the street — caressing the straggling line of vehicles . . .

Harrison's skin tingled as the raw energy of the blast touched him. He felt his body slip back, caught by the expanding circle of shock waves. The powerful concussion of the explosion held him, then tossed him aside as if he were of no consequence. He struck the snow-covered slope hard, the breath driven from his body, and rolled awkwardly to the very edge of the water. He lay stunned, ears filled by the rush of noise; the dull, flat thumps of exploding fuel tanks; the echoing thunder of the crippled aircraft coming to rest; the rumble of falling masonry; the unforgettable sounds of the dying and of the hurt and of the frightened. Harrison Bryant lay and listened to the awful sounds. Sounds that brought a touch of hell to a village named Shepthorne.

★　★　★

Consciousness returned slowly, accompanied by a dim background noise that made little sense. Mike Sandler stirred cautiously. His whole body ached — his face hurt badly, and after a while he became aware of the taste of blood in his mouth. He finally opened his eyes, and as his vision cleared his first image was one from a nightmare.

The windscreen of the radio-car had gone, shattered into a thousand fragments. Something lay across the bonnet of the car. A twisted, humped shape that he couldn't make out at first glance. Then he looked closer and a choking groan oozed from between his cut, bleeding lips.

The dark shape spread across the bonnet was all that remained of Kathy Young. Mike had finally recognised her by the colour of her hair. Some destructive force had ripped and mutilated her beautiful face and body beyond any kind of recovery. What had been a living, breathing, caring young woman only existed now as a formless mass of raw, bloodied flesh.

Mike felt a sickness rise in his throat. He tore his gaze from the butchered corpse and doubled over on the seat, vomiting on to the floor of the car. He reached out with a groping hand to open the car door, and as the door swung wide Mike let himself roll from his seat. He stumbled to his knees, throwing out his hands to brace himself. They sank wrist-deep in thick snow. Mike scooped up a handful and scrubbed it over his burning face, gasping as a thousand needlepoints of pain sprang to life. The snow in his hands turned pink from the blood flowing from the myriad cuts caused by the flying fragments of broken windscreen glass. Pushing himself unsteadily to his feet Mike leaned against the side of the car while some kind of strength returned to his trembling limbs.

Raising his head he gazed about him and saw that Shepthorne had been transformed into a wasteland of demolished buildings and wrecked vehicles. At the far end of the village — where the local garage had stood — a massive fire raged; other fires devoured the remains of shattered buildings; the skeletal shapes of gutted cars and trucks. Thick clouds of dark smoke twisted skywards in oily streamers.

Mike could make out the humped shapes of bodies strewn along the street, many of them half buried by the still falling snow; seeing them made him remember Kathy; he didn't want to think about her but the image rose unbidden in his mind. He tried to concentrate on other things. He wondered about the policeman Kathy had been speaking to — Sergeant Rodcrick. Where was *he*? Moving to the front of the estate Mike saw that the patrol car had been pushed into the front of a shop. The rear of the car was buried beneath a mass of rubble. The side of the car exposed to the street was badly dented, the paintwork blistered and shrivelled.

Something was moving slowly near the front of the car. It was a bulky figure on its hands and knees. The dark uniform hung in tatters from the bleeding body. The head hung low between the shoulders, swaying back and forth, blood dripping freely from loose strips of lacerated flesh. Mike knelt beside the figure, his hands catching hold of the man's shoulders.

'For God's sake, Roderick, what happened?'

A low, bubbling sound came from Roderick's lips. It was impossible to tell whether the man was actually speaking or simply groaning in pain.

'Roderick — it's me! Mike Sandler!'

Roderick lifted his head, his face turning up towards Mike's. The slack mouth was practically lipless, the flesh torn away to expose gums and teeth. The nose had vanished completely, leaving behind a dark, bloody cavity that pulsed with thick blood. The left eye had been torn from its socket. All that remained was a ragged hole. The other eye dangled obscenely on the end of a greasy stalk, white and glistening against the bloodied flesh of Roderick's cheek.

Mike stared about him, desperately hoping that someone would appear. He felt useless — knowing that Roderick needed help, yet aware of his own shortcomings. He caught hold of Roderick's shoulders and began to drag the moaning man away from the wrecked cars. He didn't know where the hell he was going, or what sort of help he might find, if any. He just knew he had to do *something* . . .

*   *   *

Eddie Frame held the phone in a hand that trembled visibly. He dialled 999 — then realised that the phone was dead. The lines were probably down! Damn! He let the phone drop and clambered back through the wreckage of his newsagents shop. Shoving aside bits of splintered floorboarding that had crashed down from the room above he sat down beside the half-buried body of his dead wife. He'd just have to sit and wait until the emergency services got through! They wouldn't be long! He'd have to wait — he couldn't go away and leave Ada the way she was!

*   *   *

Glass cracked under Vivian Dolby's feet as he climbed out of the shattered frontage of his gunshop and stood hesitantly on the pavement.

The first thing that caught his attention was the broken shape of the huge aircraft spread across the roadbridge at the far end of the village. Dolby let his gaze return along the street and beyond the spot he was occupying. At the other end of the street Reg Buck's garage was a blazing inferno. Closer to hand he could see flickering curls of flame rising out of the wreckage of the Shepthorne Arms Hotel, and many of the vehicles blocking the road were on fire.

Dolby shivered. It was due only in part to the cold. He began to feel the pain of his own injuries now; oddly, he hadn't noticed a thing during his removal from the rubble that had been his home. His entire body ached, with individual spots of intense pain. But from the looks of the destruction around him he was lucky to still be alive — for the present that was enough.

★   ★   ★

'Sam? Sam, where are you?'

Tearing pain in her chest made Dawn Stanton cry out. She began to struggle

66

but the effort hurt so much she almost passed out again. She fought down the panic and made herself lie very still, breathing gently. Gradually the pain lessened. Dawn stared about her, eyes wide with fear. She still didn't know what had happened. It was all a terrible blur. One minute she'd been getting dressed. There had been an odd roar of sound that had filled the room. The whole place had started to vibrate. And then the room had just fallen in; one thunderous explosion of noise and the ceiling had split wide open; the walls had swayed and collapsed; windows had shattered. There had been a choking fog of dust, confusion, noise, and finally pain as she had been thrown to the floor. More pain had followed. Dawn had passed out. When she had opened her eyes again she had found herself pinned to the floor beneath a tangled mass of splintered wood and rubble. There was something heavy across her chest, something that was hurting her, and she couldn't even move.

She'd called for Sam but he hadn't answered. For all she knew he was dead.

Or maybe hurt so badly he couldn't speak. There wasn't a thing she could do except lie still and hope that someone came looking for her and Sam very soon . . . she hoped it was soon because the pain in her chest kept coming back, stronger each time, and it was getting very, very cold.

★   ★   ★

'Please tell me what's happened,' Allison Smythe kept saying.

All Elouise could do was to tell her to stop worrying. She couldn't tell her sister any more because she didn't know any more herself. And she was too busy tending to Allison's injuries. Which wasn't easy because the house was in a terrible mess. Dust and rubble everywhere. Snow drifting in through the gaping hole in the roof. Elouise had managed to find the first-aid box but she didn't think she was going to be able to dress Allison's wounds properly.

Allison had been in the shop when the house had collapsed. She had suffered a number of cuts from flying glass. There

68

were two very bad ones that really needed stitching up as soon as possible; one in Allison's left arm, just above the elbow; the other in her face, a long, deep gash running from the corner of her left eye all the way to her jaw. Elouise had placed pads over the cuts and bandaged them in place. She was aware, however, that these could only be temporary measures. Allison had to have medical attention quickly. Luckily she was still in shock, so the pain of her wounds hadn't bothered her. But that time would come, and soon . . .

2

Ministry of Defence, London

Markfield left the lift on the 4th floor, turning down the long, starkly lit corridor. He shrugged out of his wet coat, shaking off the clinging snow with an impatient gesture. Before he reached his office the door opened and Donner stepped out, his broad young face expressing ill-concealed anger.

'Where the hell have you been?' he demanded, his voice betraying his irritation.

Walking round him Markfield went into the office. Heat from the radiators hit him like a thick woollen blanket. Markfield threw his coat down and went to the window. Easing the catch he pushed the window open. A chill gust of air drifted across his face. Snow was still falling outside and the sky was leaden. Markfield stayed where he was. He could feel

Donner's eyes boring into the back of his head.

'All right, Brian, tell me what's got you in a panic.'

Markfield sat down behind his desk while Donner opened a brown file he was holding.

'The PM has been ringing every few minutes. I've had Conrad on from Washington.'

Markfield stared at him as though he was expecting more. A hard gleam showed in Donner's eyes, and he suddenly stabbed a long finger at Markfield.

'You know all about this, don't you, Kevin?'

'It's my job to know.' Markfield picked up one of the phones on his desk and dialled a number.

'General Coreland-Smith, please. Just tell him it's Markfield. He's expecting me to call.'

Donner remained standing before Markfield's desk, tapping his fingers against the cover of the file he was holding.

'Brian, get Thompson's number at the

American Embassy. Call him and say we've got things organised. Tell him to tie up his end with the people at that airforce base — Milwich — and then if he wants he can join us and sit in . . . ' Markfield raised a hand to cut off any reply Donner might have been about to make. 'General Coreland-Smith? Kevin Markfield, sir. Are your people ready to go in?'

'They're ready, Markfield. But let me clarify something before we go any further. From what the PM said to me, I am to assume you have total control over this matter?'

'Let's say I'm responsible for dictating whatever action is necessary to achieve a satisfactory outcome.'

'That is a long-winded way of saying yes!'

Markfield grinned at the phone. 'Yes, sir.'

There was a significant grunt on the other end of the line. 'And what is my function?'

'To provide a means of completely sealing off Shepthorne. No one can be allowed to enter or leave the village. No exceptions. The village must be totally isolated. We can't allow anyone out of that village until the team arrives from Ravenswood — I cannot stress the importance of isolation . . . '

'Markfield, I understand the implications. What I am doubtful of are the motives.'

'We can discuss semantics later, General. As of this moment there is only one priority, and that is to seal off Shepthorne. Military command must be absolute.'

'To what degree?'

Markfield sighed; he'd been anticipating that question ever since Coreland-Smith had come on the line.

'If force has to be used to implement your orders then it must be employed.'

'Very well, Markfield. I'll get my people moving.'

'Thank you, sir.' Markfield put the phone down.

Downing Street, London

'Please keep me informed of all developments, Kevin,' the PM said, then added:

'Let us hope we have acted quickly enough.'

The PM broke the connection, pressed a button, and waited until the holding line had been opened.

'Mr President, the matter is now in hand. We will do everything humanly possible to redress this unfortunate accident.'

'If there is anything you need, any assistance we can give, please do not hesitate to contact me.'

'Hopefully our efforts will suffice. The problem is we are dealing with a totally unknown quantity. Under those circumstances all we can do now is wait.'

* * *

The big Range Rover, lights flashing and siren howling, careered along the road with an almost reckless disregard for the long line of stalled vehicles that had backed up from Shepthorne. It swept by in a spray of thick snow, only slowing when it reached the section of road that had been cleared on the outskirts of the village. Almost before it had stopped the passenger door opened and a tall, uniformed figure jumped out and hurried across to the waiting group of policemen.

'Anything fresh to tell me?' the newcomer snapped.

Sergeant Bob Manning shrugged. 'Nothing you haven't already heard, sir.'

'I thought you'd have it all cleared up by now, Bob,' Inspector Ronald Henderson said.

Manning smiled. 'No miracles on a Monday, sir.'

'Let's go and have a closer look,' Henderson suggested. He led the way over to his Range Rover. As he reached the vehicle he turned to the other policemen. 'The emergency services should be arriving shortly. I don't want any holdups. Get a way cleared along that road even if you have to push those damn cars and trucks in the ditch!'

Henderson opened the driver's door and waved the officer out of the seat. 'Take over Sergeant Morley's car while he's supervising the road clearance. Make contact with HQ. I want an open channel at all times. Sergeant Manning and I are going to have a closer look at the village.'

As Manning settled in the passenger seat Henderson gunned the powerful motor and took the Range Rover in the direction of the village. More abandoned vehicles lined the deserted road. Henderson drove steadily, peering through the falling snow. As the Range Rover rounded a curve they were able to see the orange glow of flames and the dark smudges of thick smoke smeared across the sky.

'I can't understand the difficulty we seem to be having every time we try and find out about this bloody aircraft,' Manning said. 'It must belong to somebody.'

'It does, but nobody wants to own up,' Henderson said. 'A thing that size can't come down and not be missed.'

Ahead the road was blocked. There was no way through for the Range Rover. Henderson pulled the vehicle to a halt. He turned up the collar of his parka and opened the door. Before Manning got out he picked up the radio-phone and contacted base communications to let them know that they were leaving the Range Rover unattended.

The two policemen made their way along the road. As they got closer to the final approach to the village evidence of the initial destruction became apparent.

Burned-out vehicles blocked the narrow road. Blackened, windowless, their tyres melted by the intense heat, the bodywork ripped open from exploding fuel tanks. Smoke drifted up from many of the gutted wrecks. Here and there flame still ate at dripping plastic. Trees and hedges along the side of the road had been shrivelled by the heat. The snow was dark with soot and charred debris.

Many of the vehicles still contained the remains of their drivers and passengers. Black, skeletal figures still in their seats. Flesh burned away, tissue and muscle shrunken, they remained like dark spectres, silently observing the desolate scene through blind eyes set in black, grimacing skulls.

Manning glanced at his superior. 'Poor sods,' he murmured.

Raising his eyes from other bodies lying in the thick snow Henderson said: 'maybe they were the lucky ones. The way that fireball must have hit them it would have been over in seconds. What we have to find out now is how many there are still in that village. Alive but maybe badly hurt. And how the hell are we going to get the emergency services through to them?'

Unzipping his parka Manning produced his personal-communicator.

'Four-zero-nine to Mobile Control. Over.'

The handset crackled and then a voice came through. 'Mobile to four-zero-nine. Receiving you. Over.'

'Inspector Henderson and I are just entering the village. I'll keep you informed on what we find. Can you give me information on situation regarding emergency services? Over.'

'Mobile to four-zero-nine. Emergency services are having difficulty getting to us because of heavy traffic blocking road. We're attempting to clear a way for them. Will keep you informed. Over.'

'Thank you Mobile. Four-zero-nine. Out.'

They carried on along the road. At the

bend in the road where it entered Shepthorne they were forced to climb over the fence and tramp through a field before emerging on the edge of the village. At that spot the road was completely blocked by a wedge of burned-out vehicles. The heat from the fireball had been so intense that the bodyshells of the cars and trucks had softened and twisted out of shape.

The garage still burned. The forecourt was a blackened expanse of cracked concrete. Where the storage tanks had exploded the forecourt had been ripped open. The remains of the tanker lay on its side. Yards away the twisted shape of another truck lay half buried under shattered concrete.

Henderson gazed along the devastated street, taking in the bodies. The rubble. The utter destruction. The distant but dominating shape of the crashed aircraft. He shook his head slowly.

'Where the hell do you start sorting out a mess like this?'

* * *

Vivian Dolby was limping cautiously along the street when he saw the two policemen. He lifted an arm to attract their attention.

'Over here!' he called.

'It's Major Dolby, isn't it, sir?' said the taller of the two policemen.

Dolby stared at the man for a moment. His mind seemed to have slowed down. Then recognition came. 'Inspector Henderson. It's good to see a familiar face.'

The second policeman caught hold of Dolby's arm as the major swayed unsteadily.

'Are you hurt, Major?' Henderson asked.

'Took a nasty bang on the head just as the house caved in. I must admit it aches a little.'

'I'm afraid there isn't much we can do for you at the moment, Major,' Henderson apologized. 'We're having problems getting the emergency services through.'

'Don't worry about me, Inspector,' Dolby said. He made a conscious effort to stand erect despite the way he felt. 'There must be others much worse off than me.'

Henderson spotted movement further up the street.

'There — two people.'

The policemen moved towards the advancing figures, Dolby following slowly. By the time he caught up to them they were standing over the bloody form of Sergeant Roderick.

' . . . and Kathy was dead . . . ' Mike Sandler was saying.

'Major, would you give a hand, and we'll try to move Sergeant Roderick to a safe place,' Henderson said.

Dolby stared at the pitiful wreck that had been Roderick and his stomach began to heave. He fought the sensation down. 'Anything I can do to help,' he said.

Mike Sandler insisted on helping too, ignoring his own injuries.

Henderson took Sergeant Manning aside. 'See they get clear of the village. I want to take a closer look at that aircraft.'

'Watch out for yourself, sir. If that thing catches fire . . . '

'That's why I want to check it.'

⋆ ⋆ ⋆

Melted snow trickled icily down inside his clothes, making his flesh cringe as he sat up. Harrison Bryant swore softly. Jesus, it was cold! His teeth were chattering, making an idiotic sound that he couldn't control. He stared about him, desperately trying to coordinate his senses.

The village was in ruins. Buildings wrecked, some with flames rising from the heaped piles of rubble. Smoke hung thickly over the desolate scene. Cars and trucks were strewn along the street, many of them burned-out wrecks. There was a battered, blistered truck standing no more than a dozen yards from where he sat in the snow.

Harrison stood up — very slowly — until he was sure there were no broken bones or damaged organs. Satisfied, he straightened up and found he was trembling violently. His head ached. Apart from that he seemed fine.

Up at the far end of the village part of a burning building collapsed. Flame and smoke billowed upwards. A shower of bright sparks hissed across the snow-filled sky.

Harrison took a step up the slope.

And behind him a girl's voice asked: 'Would you help me — please!'

He turned around.

A Triumph TR7 sports car, bodywork badly damaged, was perched on the very edge of the riverbank. The car's front was partly submerged in the dark water of the river, pulled down by the dead weight of the engine. As Harrison neared the car he saw it move. It slipped forward an inch or so, the front sinking a little deeper in the water. Bubbles rose noisily to the surface. Oil from the engine floated into sight, making multicoloured rings. There was movement inside the car. Harrison leaned over. The driver's window was wound halfway down and he could see the scared white face of a pretty young woman staring out at him.

Harrison grabbed hold of the door handle and tried to pull it open. The door refused to budge. He braced one foot against the side of the car and tried again. Stepping back he saw that the rear section of the body was twisted out of shape, locking the door solidly in its frame.

Jenny Morrish brushed strands of dark hair away from her pale face. 'I'm afraid my foot's trapped.' There was a faint tremor in her voice when she added: 'The car seems to be sinking. The water in here is getting higher all the time . . . and it's damn cold!'

Harrison grinned at her last remark. 'I'll see what I can do about getting you out.'

★ ★ ★

Inspector Henderson craned his neck as he gazed at the tangled mass of metal curving above him. At a conservative estimate he guessed that the aircraft must have been around eighty to ninety feet in length. Even now, broken and lifeless, it dominated its immediate surroundings by its sheer bulk. The still-falling snow had begun to cover it, but Henderson was able to decipher the markings on sections of the fuselage and wings.

The aircraft belonged to the United States Airforce. It looked like some kind of transport. Henderson read off all the numbers and letters painted on the high tail section, which was still intact, and wrote them down on a pad from his pocket. Maybe he'd be able to track down who was responsible for the damn thing!

Forward of the crumpled nose section Henderson could see that access across the stone bridge was impossible. The foresection of the bulbous fuselage lay squarely on the bridge, overlapping on either side. They weren't going to bring in any emergency vehicles by that route.

Henderson became aware of a strong smell of aviation fuel. He walked back along the length of the aircraft, passing beneath one of the main wings. It didn't take him long to locate the leak. Fuel was streaming from a jagged rent in the wing's outer skin. It had already begun to pool on the ground. There was no way of knowing just how much fuel the aircraft was carrying, but it was a safe bet there would be enough to cause a big blaze if it did ignite. Henderson thought about the fires in the damaged buildings. If they weren't brought under control soon they would spread, reaching down to the houses at this end of the village. Once that happened it wouldn't take very much — just a few sparks in the right place — and then they would have more problems. Added to that was the fact that no one yet knew what, if anything, the aircraft was carrying as cargo. It was entirely feasible that it might hold a cargo of explosives; after all it *was* a military aircraft.

Turning away from the aircraft Henderson tramped back through the filthy snow, making his way to the point where he and Manning had entered Shepthorne.

He couldn't afford to wait for the emergency services arriving. The main thing to attend to was the evacuation of the village. Get everyone they could out of the place. Then worry about the possibility of further fires or explosions. Henderson decided to bring in as many of his men as possible. Get them to go through the damaged houses and bring out anyone they found. It was going to take time — and time was something they were short of, but it was a positive move.

★ ★ ★

Smithy — it was his first and last name, the only one he would ever answer to — was by nature a man motivated by total self-interest. He saw everything as being potentially opportune to some degree; his initial reaction in any situation was to calculate how he could profit through it. He lived alone in a small cottage, situated some four miles from Shepthorne. From there Smithy conducted his solitary and selfish existence. By various means — mainly devious — he scraped a living which kept him fed, clothed, and more or less supplied with everything he needed.

One of Smithy's preoccupations was poaching. He wasn't a particularly good poacher, but he was adept enough at it to provide himself with a steady diet of fresh meat and poultry, sometimes even the odd fish. The trouble was that Smithy was also a lazy man, and he had allowed his laxity to linger to the point where his reserves were practically non-existent. He was out that day looking for food, with a growing feeling he wasn't going to find any, and freezing into the bargain.

Nothing had gone the way he'd planned. The weather was cold. The snowstorm continued unabated. Smithy tramped the fields, his shotgun under his arm, muffled up to the eyeballs in an old army greatcoat. He hadn't seen one damn rabbit. Come to that he hadn't seen another living thing. After a couple of hours he was ready to pack it in. The way things were going he might have to do something really desperate — such as actually *buying* his food for the next few days. The thought made him feel distinctly uncomfortable. Smithy disliked having to work to earn money — he disliked even more having to spend the stuff once he'd got it.

His mind was trying to come to terms with the evils of the capitalist system, and was so absorbed that Smithy didn't become aware of the noise for some time. But it became so strong that it penetrated his train of thought and forced him to seek out the source.

The source turned out to be the biggest aircraft Smithy had ever seen in his life. What was more terrifying was that it was flying extremely low and sinking even lower with each second. Smithy stood paralysed. He watched open-mouthed as the aircraft swept in over the snowy fields and ripped a destructive swathe the length of Shepthorne.

From his vantage point on a low line of hills overlooking the village Smithy saw the whole thing. It was almost like watching some wide-screen film spectacular on a gigantic canvas. He flinched when the huge fireball engulfed Reg Buck's garage and then rolled out along the village street. More explosions followed as fuel tanks ignited, and burning vehicles lined the debris-filled street. He viewed the aircraft's final moments of flight, then its jarring impact as it came to rest across the old stone bridge. For a while there was noise and brilliant light, and then gradually a bleak silence fell over the stricken village.

Smithy sank on to his haunches and stared down on the village. After a while a slow smile began to play around the edges of his mouth. He rubbed a grubby hand across his unshaven jaw. An ugly gleam showed in his cold eyes. His mind was working swiftly now, as he saw before him the chance for a quick killing. There was going to be chaos in the village for some time. People would be confused, hurt, not aware of their surroundings. They would be too busy looking after themselves to be bothered about material things. Smithy began to grin. Down there in Shepthorne were shops and shops contained goods. Now a man using his wits might slip in and out of those damaged buildings, helping himself to whatever he fancied. Smithy climbed to his feet and began to make his way towards Shepthorne. He moved swiftly, in a wide loop that would bring him in at the rear of the main street. If he took his time, kept his eyes open, he could be in and out of that place before anyone could possibly spot him. He began to think it might not be such a bad day after all.

It took him a couple of hours to reach the wooded stretch of land behind the village. Crouching in the undergrowth Smithy listened and looked. It was still pretty quiet. He'd spotted one or two people moving about but he'd expected that. There was still a lot of smoke from the various fires that still burned. Combined with the falling snow it created a curtain of mist that would help to mask his movements.

He was near the top end of the village. From where he was crouched Smithy could see the high tail of the crashed aircraft rising above the nearby rooftops. Christ, it was even bigger close up, he realised. His curiosity drew him along the undergrowth, bringing him nearer the aircraft. Now he could see the markings on the fuselage. It was an American plane! Smithy felt his inside coil up with excitement. American meant money: it was a simple equation as far as Smithy was concerned. He could imagine all kinds of things inside that aircraft. He wondered what kind of cargo it was carrying. There was only one way to find out. He could do the shops later. It was worth spending a few minutes checking the plane over first. Never know what he might pick up!

Smithy crept along the thick under-growth until he was level with the aircraft. The wing above his head had been ripped open. There was a strong petrol-like smell in the air. Probably spilled fuel, he thought. He edged out of the under-growth and scuttled across the short stretch of open ground separating him from the aircraft. Smithy knelt beside it, leaning a shoulder against the fuselage. He ran a hand across the cold metal. There'd be a few quid for scrap in this little pile! He looked for a way in. Some feet to his left he spotted an opening. It looked like some kind of emergency hatch — probably sprung open when the aircraft had hit the ground. Smithy leaned his head and shoulders inside. There was a huge tear in the fuselage on the other side, high up, so there was plenty of light streaming in.

Grunting with the effort Smithy dragged himself through the hatch and peered around him. Almost immediately disappointment showed in his face. The bloody thing was empty! The huge cargo space, littered with debris from the shattered fuselage, was bare! There wasn't a bit of cargo at all. Not a sodding, solitary . . .

Yes there is, Smithy boy!

He approached it slowly, scratching his head as he tried to figure out what it was. Some kind of frame bolted to the floor. No more than three feet high and a couple of feet square. On top was a solid-looking metal box made of a dull material. It appeared to have a lid that was fastened down by metal snap-fasteners, two on each side. Smithy put down his shotgun and began to loosen the fasteners. When he'd freed the last one he took hold of the lid-section and yanked it free. There was a thick lining inside — some kind of dense, absorbent rubber. And nestling in the centre of that rubbery cocoon was a thick metal cylinder. At first glance it looked very like a cigar-tube; but it was too large for that. Smithy reckoned it was at least a foot and a half long and seven or eight inches round. Near one end there was a groove cut into the cylinder. Smithy decided that would be where the cap unscrewed; it seemed logical; there had to be a way to get inside the thing. He reached out to pick the cylinder up. His fingers touched the smooth metal. Smithy jerked his hand back. It was cold — but more than that it felt wet. He peered at his fingers. He could make out a sheen of glistening moisture. He rubbed the tips of his fingers together; the stuff had a faintly slimy feel to it. He rubbed his hands together and the wetness seemed to disappear. Smithy lost interest in the cylinder. It didn't look as if it was of any use to him after all. He turned and made his way back along the metal walkway. Maybe he could pick something up in the control cabin. The crew must have had things in their pockets.

When he dragged the buckled door open and peered into the control cabin he wished he hadn't. Whatever the crew might have been carrying in their pockets would have to stay there. Smithy stared at the pulped and bloody remains of the crew and began to feel very sick; despite his revulsion he couldn't tear his eyes from the mutilated, crushed, ripped bodies of what had been men only a short while ago; the buckled and sheared metal of the flight deck was streaked and splashed with gouts of blood; splintered white bone grinned starkly out of mashed flesh; incredibly long intestinal tubes snaked greasily across the bloody floor panels.

Smithy dragged himself away from the door and staggered to the open hatch. He crouched and slithered out of the aircraft. When his feet touched the ground his legs weakened and he sprawled face down in the snow. He lay for a while. God, but he felt terrible! He sat up. His head was beginning to pound and a nauseous sensation swelled up from his stomach. Damn, he thought, I wish I hadn't seen them dead buggers! He stood, slowly, unsure of himself, and had to lean against the side of the aircraft. The nausea swirled around in his stomach. He began to heave uncontrollably. The contents of his stomach rose in his throat, spilling from his mouth in a deluge. Even when there was nothing left to bring up he continued to retch, each convulsion of his stomach muscles bringing pain. The retching subsided after a couple of long, agonised minutes. Smithy dragged air into his lungs. He felt weak now and the pain in his head was increasing. What the hell was wrong with him? He pushed away from the side of the aircraft, wanting suddenly to be far removed from the thing.

He stumbled and lurched back into the thick undergrowth, falling often. He wasn't even aware that he'd left his shotgun behind in the aircraft. If he had it wouldn't have meant very much to him. Smithy was hurting too much, and he couldn't understand why. Over the next few minutes he dragged himself deep into the dense wood. Finally he found he couldn't move any further. He stared around him, blinking away the tears that seemed to be constantly filling his eyes. The place was somehow familiar. There was a small stream close by he recalled. Yes — there it was! He pulled himself to the edge and bent over to take a drink. Thinking about the stream had made him aware of how thirsty he'd become. His throat felt swollen, tight.

Something made him pause, made him

stare at his reflection in the water. For a moment he felt sure he was imagining things. That wasn't *his* face in the water. He leaned closer. A hoarse rattle rose in his swollen throat. It *was* his face . . . but what had happened to it? What had . . . Smithy noticed his left hand resting on the edge of the bank. He raised it in front of his eyes.

'Christ!'

He stared, horrified, at a hand undergoing some terrible change almost before his eyes. Flesh turning brown and yellow, puckering and swelling into bulging pustules. The finger joints stiffening as the tissue around them filled out, ballooning grotesquely. A similar metamorphosis was taking effect across the strained features of his face; Smithy's mind absorbed the fact but there was no capacity for acceptance. Summoning a hidden reserve of strength, fed through fear, he lurched to his feet and began to run. It was an aimless flight, generated by the pain he was suffering and amplified by the fact that he was in total ignorance of what was happening to him.

* ★ *

The three helicopters swept in from the west, sliding in from the pale sky and losing height as they closed in on the area surrounding Shepthorne. Previously they had flown in a tight formation but now, as if on some programmed course, they broke apart. One made its landing to the south of the village, touching down in a field just beyond the dense wood at the rear of Shepthorne; the second landed on the far side of the river, close to the approach road to the village; the remaining helicopter drifted groundwards as close to the blocked stone bridge as it could get.

Each helicopter disgorged over a dozen armed and heavily equipped soldiers. In addition to their automatic weapons and packs, the soldiers wore all-enveloping protective suits complete with visored hoods and air-filtration units. Each group fanned out to form a long line — eventually forming a ragged circle that had Shepthorne as its centre-point. The combined force began to close in on the village. The intention was clear — to surround and isolate Shepthorne . . .

'All right, Sergeant, have the unit secure all positions. And just make certain that every man knows what he has to do! We can't afford any mistakes!'

Sergeant Andy Duggan sleeved sweat from his face; despite the low temperature outside he was uncomfortably warm inside the constricting suit — it had been a relief to remove the visored hood, even though it was only a temporary measure.

'They'll do what's needed, sir,' he promised: to himself he added — if they don't *I'll* want to know why!

Captain Mather stared out through the open door of the command helicopter, gazing at the bulk of the huge aircraft. The initial urgency of the operation — assembly of the unit and their equipment followed by the flight to Shepthorne — had left little time for any kind of deliberations. Now, with arrival behind him and the unit deployed, Mather found time to gather his thoughts, and he became aware of worrying implications behind the orders he'd been given. Peter Mather was a professional soldier, trained to accept any given situation and to act accordingly. During his career Mather had faced a number of difficult situations: confrontations that had been resolved without any kind of personal soul-searching. This operation was different. He was expected to secure control of a village here in his own country, and to effect absolute military authority to the limit, using force if necessary to stabilise the situation. Mather's commanding officer, General Coreland-Smith, had given orders in such a manner that Mather was in no doubt as to the importance of the operation. Yet there was still a nagging worry at the back of Mather's mind. Faced with a determined enemy in a tactical situation Mather would have been in no doubt as to where his duty lay. Here, today, in this snowbound village, not yet certain what he might be called upon to do, he found difficulty in justifying Coreland-Smith's directive.

Behind Mather the radio crackled into life. The corporal in charge of it eased out of his seat and handed Mather a message-sheet.

'Damn!' Mather crumpled the sheet with an angry gesture.

'Trouble, sir?' Duggan asked.

'They've got problems getting those bloody people in from Ravenswood! That means we'll have to keep the lid on this mess longer than anticipated.'

'That's all we need,' Duggan said. 'Here we are sitting on top of God knows what and . . . '

Mather cut him off. He pointed to the far side of the bridge, beyond the crashed aircraft. A uniformed figure was tramping through the thick snow in a slow, but direct line that would eventually bring him to the bridge . . .

Picking up his uniform cap Mather put it on. He glanced at his sergeant. 'Chin up, Duggan, let's go and see what the local constabulary wants.'

*　*　*

Private Larry Kemp was already scared.

It had been a big mistake his joining the army. He'd realised that within the first few months. Basic training had been

101

hard but he'd got through it. It was afterwards, when the novelty of the whole thing had started to wear off, that Kemp found he wasn't cut out for soldiering. The trouble was it had been too late to back out. He'd signed on, and getting out was a bloody sight harder than getting in.

'You could always shoot off a big toe,' one of his mates told him. 'Or anything else you wouldn't miss!'

Kemp had realised it wasn't a good idea to broadcast the fact that he hated the army and everybody in it. Come the day he handed in his uniform he could tell them all to stuff it! Until he worked out some way of getting his discharge he still had to live and work among all the other men, so it would be stupid to alienate them. He decided to keep his mouth shut.

The problem was that his dislike of the army and its system made it difficult to put up with the daily grind. He found it harder and harder to keep up the expected standard, to follow the rules and regulations. He became obsessed with the idea that if he didn't get out of the army something bad was going to happen. Like getting shot. Or blown up. Or . . . The obsession became a nightmare that stayed with him awake or asleep. It slowly, inexorably shredded his nerves until Kemp was drawn closer and closer to breaking point.

And that breaking point had never been nearer than the day that placed him in Shepthorne.

He hadn't understood the need for the abrupt mounting of the operation. Or the sinister meaning behind the protective suits. It was only as he found himself patrolling the outskirts of the village, aware of the awful destruction, the broken shape of that huge aircraft at the far end of the street, that his misgivings gave way to wild speculation, and he allowed his flitting fantasies to form into ugly facts.

There was something on that plane! Something dangerous! And anybody who went near it would probably die. That was why they were wearing the suits!

Kemp halted. He stood there and stared about him. This was bloody crazy!

He shouldn't be here. He didn't want to be here.

Well, he wasn't going to let them kill him! They could do what they wanted but he wasn't going near that bloody plane! No way was he going near the thing!

He began to shiver. It was cold. The ground underfoot lay deep in thick mud, layered by a carpet of snow. It was difficult to walk in a straight line. His boots kept slipping and sliding. Kemp heard a distant voice. He glanced across the field and saw a figure, dressed in a suit similar to his own, coming towards him.

'Come on, Kemp, shape up!'

Even through the muffling visor Kemp recognised the sharp tone of Sergeant Wendover.

'It ain't easy walkin' in this stuff,' Kemp moaned.

'You drop back again, lad, and I'll put my boot up your arse! Then you won't have to worry about walking — because your feet won't be touching the ground!'

Kemp curled his lip behind the protection of his visor. He stumbled on, at odds with his surroundings, with himself and with the world in general.

* * *

Acrid dust soured Sam Mayhew's throat. He blinked as more dust sifted down into his eyes. He was getting angry, and when Sam got angry he lost control of sense and reason. At other times that had proved to be a stumbling block. It had created a bad image, something the bank frowned upon; as with most august and venerable institutions it was extremely conscious of its image, and had little patience with anyone who broke the traditions of decades. Luckily for Sam he possessed a unique acumen within the sphere of banking activities that allowed his peccadillos to be overlooked; he knew though that his playing around with Dawn, if it reached the attention of his board, would be viewed differently. Sam was a married man, with three children; the odd display of bad temper could be forgotten — a deliberate and constant abandoning of fidelity could not. The thought flashed through Sam's mind as he lay in the ruins of the room, and it stirred him to action.

He was still pinned to the floor by some damn weight across his shoulders. When he tried to move he heard ominous creaking sounds all around him. Dust and debris showered over him. But he refused to just lie there. For one thing nobody seemed to be coming to look for him. Whatever had happened seemed to have paralysed the whole village. He was still unsure of just what had taken place. All he could recall was the initial noise. The explosions. The room falling in. Then a period of blackness. Coming round slowly to a background of noise; cries and screams; the roar of flames; there had been a smell of smoke from somewhere close by. Maybe the damn hotel was burning!

Sam got both hands against the floor. He took a deep breath and began to push up against the dead weight on his shoulders. After a time he relaxed. Sweat trickled down his face. He couldn't be sure but he felt a little freer. As if he'd moved the thing off his shoulders a fraction. He rested for a couple of minutes. Then he tried again. This time he put everything into the effort. The muscles of his chest and shoulders and arms began to ache. There was a sharp pain in his left shoulder where something hard thrust against the flesh. Sam ignored the pain and allowed anger to add to his strength. His arms were trembling, threatening to give under the strain, when he felt the solid weight begin to slide. It eased to one side, debris pattering to the floor around Sam. He gathered himself and made a final upward heave. The weight slid clear, crashing to the floor. More debris, shaken loose by the sudden collapse, showered down over Sam, and for a moment he thought he was going to end up buried again, but he managed to get his feet under him, limping away from the avalanche of falling masonry and splintered beams that thundered to the floor. Dust boiled up in grey clouds, making him cough. Sam stumbled across the rubble-strewn floor of the room.

He halted abruptly, staring.

There in front of him, half buried by a mass of debris, was Dawn. He could see her head and shoulders. One arm. The main part of her body was covered. Her left leg protruded from the debris — or what remained of her left leg; from the knee down it was terribly mutilated, the flesh torn and pulped, exposing the very bone; it made Sam sick just to look at it.

He moved closer to Dawn, not sure whether she was alive or not. Her eyes were open, wide and staring. Her mouth sagged and there was blood trickling from one corner. The right cheek was badly bruised and swollen.

'Oh, Sam, I'm so glad you've come!' she said suddenly. 'I thought you'd gone without me . . . '

★   ★   ★

Inspector Henderson waited with uncon-cealed impatience at the approach of the two soldiers. He was an angry man. Puzzled too, by the sudden and menacing appearance of the military. Their attitude had left Henderson frustrated, impotent, his authority ignored, and he needed an excuse to express his disgust.

'Captain,' he said, 'there had better be a damn good reason for the behaviour of your men!'

Peter Mather refused to be intimidated by Henderson's icy stare. 'Inspector, my authority overrides any other in this area — including yours. I have my orders and so have my men. Those orders state that there will be no kind of interference with the duties of my group.'

'Just what are your *duties*, Captain?' Henderson queried. 'Do they include intimidation of emergency services attempting to bring assistance to injured people?'

'They are not my concern!'

Henderson stared at him as if he couldn't believe what he'd heard. 'I'd like to think you hadn't said that.' He stabbed a finger in the direction of the wrecked buildings. 'There are people in there,' he yelled. 'Hurt — some of them dying probably. In this weather a lot of them aren't going to survive for very long. Or hadn't you noticed how bloody cold it is?'

'Inspector, I can do nothing for them.'

'Can't or won't?' Henderson asked. 'Anyway, I'm not asking you for any help. Just let my people into the village to pull the injured out of this mess. Give us a chance to bring the emergency services in. We won't interfere with you.'

Mather shook his head. 'It can't be done!'

'Then at least have the decency to tell me why, man! I'm not stupid, Captain. It's to do with that aircraft. What's so bloody important you'll commit murder to protect it?'

'Murder?' Mather flinched slightly.

Henderson smiled tightly. 'That's what it'll be if anyone dies in this village because of your damned orders, *Captain*!'

Mather held himself motionless for a long moment. Then he glanced at the sergeant who had accompanied him. 'Sergeant Duggan, have the inspector escorted out of the village. Then post six men around the aircraft. I want them twenty-five yards clear of the thing. No one goes near it.'

Duggan nodded. 'Holland!' he yelled. An armed private came over. 'All right, Inspector, let's go.'

Henderson hesitated, watching the retreating figure of the young captain. His hesitation earned him a poke in the ribs from the muzzle of the rifle being carried by the private.

'Sir!' Duggan's tone was respectful but determined.

They walked away from the bridge, leaving the awesome bulk of the crippled aircraft behind them. Duggan called over a solider wearing the stripes of a corporal and gave orders for the posting of guards around the Hercules.

Aware of the rifle directed at his back Henderson followed the sergeant along the debris-strewn street. Drifting smoke from one of the smouldering buildings stung their eyes and rasped in their throats.

'Sergeant, I don't understand what this is all about. Can't you give me some idea?'

'I'd expect you to know better than to ask that, sir,' Duggan said without even looking back.

Henderson stopped dead in his tracks. He reached out and caught hold of Duggan's sleeve, pulling the man round to face him. 'Cut out the James Bond nonsense, Sergeant Duggan, and try to give me a straight answer! Just why are you people deliberately cutting off this village from the outside world? And what is it you're hiding on that plane?'

'Inspector, why won't *you* just do as you're told?' Duggan asked wearily.

'Because, damnit, I don't like what I see.'

'Hard luck!' Duggan said. 'Now move!'

Henderson's control snapped and he shoved the sergeant aside. Too late he remembered the armed soldier at his back. He tried to step out of the way. Heard a rustle of sound. Then felt something smash into his left side. The force of the blow drove him to his knees, pain flaring, a sickness making him break out in a cold sweat. He found it hard to breathe. His side burned with pain.

'On your feet, *sir*!'

Henderson clamped his lips shut against the anger threatening to spill out in verbal abuse. He stood up, gasping for breath, feeling the pain stab at him. He wondered if any ribs were broken.

'Don't do anything like that again,' Duggan warned. 'Just walk on and don't stop until I tell you to!'

★　★　★

'I don't understand what's happening,' Elouise said. 'When I saw those soldiers I thought they were here to help. Now I'm not sure they are.' She hesitated. 'After the way I just saw them treat that nice Inspector Henderson . . . '

She stopped talking, aware of Allison's listless stare. Elouise sighed. She was rather confused, unsure of the meaning behind the events of the past few hours. One thing Elouise *was* certain of — she had no intention of putting Allison and herself into the care of the soldiers. At least not until she had a clearer indication of their intentions. It worried her because she wanted to get Allison to a doctor. Her sister was badly hurt and the cold wasn't helping at all.

She turned to Allison and made sure that her sister was still well wrapped up in the blankets she'd managed to rescue from the rubble of their home.

★ ★ ★

Avoiding looking at Kathy's corpse on the bonnet of the radio-car, Mike Sandler eased open the driver's door and slid inside. The smell from his own vomit still lingered. He picked up the mike and slipped on the headset, flicking switches to turn on the transmitter.

'Jerry?'

'Where the hell have you been? I've talked myself bloody hoarse trying to raise you pair for the last . . . '

'Listen, Jerry.'

'I know you fancy Kathy — but couldn't you wait 'til the programme's over . . . '

'For Christ sake, Jerry, shut up and listen!' Mike yelled. 'Kathy's dead!'

Silence.

'There was a plane crash. Some great American thing. It came down on the village. Tore down most of the buildings. There've been fires. Explosions. Cars on fire and a lot of people dead. Probably more injured.'

'What about . . . I mean Kathy?'

'I was inside the car. Kathy had gone out to tape an interview with one of the local coppers. Then it . . . just happened. All I remember was this bloody great bang. It got hot, and that was it until I woke up and found . . .'

'Hell, I'm sorry, Mike . . . What're things like?'

'It's weird. The whole village has been ringed by the army. They're everywhere. They're refusing to allow anyone to leave and they won't let the emergency services in.'

'They give a reason?'

'According to them they don't need one. All they're interested in is sealing this place off!'

'Can you pick anything up?'

Mike's reply was slow in coming. 'I'll see what I can do, Jerry. You — er — hang on and I'll get back to you.' He switched off the transmitter and removed the headset. Then he climbed slowly out of the radio-car, never once taking his eyes from the threatening black muzzles of the two rifles aimed at him — rifles that were held by impassive soldiers who stared at him from behind the transparent visors of their protective hoods.

★   ★   ★

It had taken a long time to get the driver's door on the TR7 open. Harrison Bryant's fingers were raw and bleeding, and he'd almost given up hope. Despite his misgivings he carried on attacking the jammed door with the iron tyre-lever he'd found under the seat of the burned-out truck standing nearby. He could still see the awful sight that had been exposed to him on opening the truck door — the dead driver hunched over the wheel, bony fingers still gripping the melted plastic rim — the charred jaw opened wide to bare yellowed teeth sunk in black gums — the blistered flesh of the burned body melted away to the bones by the fierce heat . . . Tearing his eyes from the corpse Harrison had fumbled under the seat, eventually closing his fingers around the tyre-lever.

The door of the TR7 opened with a snap. Harrison stumbled awkwardly as the tension was removed from the lever He jammed one end of the iron into the ground, then closed both hands over the edge of the door. He dragged it open against the resistance of badly twisted hinges.

'Now we come to the easy part,' he grinned.

'Are you always so cheerful?' Jenny asked.

'Well, to judge that you'd have to see me first thing in a morning. Over the breakfast table.'

A slow smile edged across Jenny's pale face. 'I've had some offers in my time,' she said, 'but that was about the best.'

'Is it a date?'

'You get me out of this car,' Jenny said, 'and you can have the night before the morning after!'

Before either of them could speak again the TR7 began to slide further into the water, the front sinking even deeper. Chilled water bubbled up over Jenny's knees. She gave a frightened cry as the car slid to one side.

As the car started to move Harrison caught hold of the doorframe and attempted to halt the forward movement. His booted feet slithered across the soft ground. He thrust his heels in deeply, heaving against the car's dead weight until his muscles creaked.

Abruptly the movement ceased. The TR7 rocked slowly. Air bubbles rose up through the water around Jenny's legs. She sat rigid in her seat, hardly daring to breathe in case it started the car moving again. When she felt Harrison's hand touch hers she grasped it tightly, and he could feel her trembling violently.

'Do you realise something?' Jenny said finally, her voice very low. 'I don't even know your name!'

Harrison stared at her and smiled. 'Harrison Bryant.'

'Well I'm very glad to meet you, Harrison Bryant. I'm Jenny Morrish.'

Smithy's sense of direction was nullified. His objectivity had become lost in the overwhelming spread of pain. Thought — action — response — had no deliberate motivation. The pain was supreme. Complete. And becoming unbearable . . .

He found himself stumbling through piles of rubble; shattered bricks and splintered beams. He fell often, opening ugly gashes in his face and body. Smithy ignored them, moving on, weaving his uncertain path towards — where he didn't know . . .

A door blocked his way. Smithy stared at it through watering eyes. The flesh around them was swollen, the bulging rolls almost concealing his pupils. His bloated lips moved, forming an ugly snarl. He lurched forward, hurling himself at the barrier before him, and the weakened door tore free from its hinges, spilling Smithy headlong into the half-demolished room beyond.

Almost buried beneath piles of debris lay a dead woman. A man sat beside her, holding a cold, lifeless hand in his own. The man glanced across the shattered room. He saw the figure sprawled in the rubble. Watched it climb to its feet.

'Who are . . . ?' The question died on Eddie Frame's lips. He shuddered in revulsion at the nightmare that stumbled across the room towards him.

The bulging pustules covering Smithy's face and body had burst and thick pus pulsed from them. The decaying flesh lay exposed, raw and weeping. Smithy reached out with bloody, festered hands as he neared the man cowering on the floor.

Eddie Frame abandoned his dead wife, his grief wiped away in an instant. The fear of something he couldn't understand jolted him into movement, and he scrambled backwards in a desperate attempt to gain some distance between himself and the shambling, suffering effigy of a man. When he tried to stand he felt his right leg give; it was stiff with cramp, caused by his sitting immobile for too long. Eddie fell, gashing a hand badly on some broken glass. Ignoring the injury he tried to stand again. He had to keep away from the bloated thing which seemed determined to reach him.

Smithy — unable to speak through swollen vocal chords — was driven by some deep inner need to communicate. A faint spark still burned, a small reminder of his own personality . . . to survive he had to make contact . . .

Smithy made the universal gesture of friendship. He put out a hand. All he wanted to do was to show Eddie Frame he meant him no harm. He reached out and he touched Eddie's own hand.

And with that simple gesture he unwittingly killed Eddie Frame.

* ★ ★

'I don't give a damn what your reasons are, Markfield. You can't just walk in and close this station down!'

Kevin Markfield glanced out of the office window. Thick snow, driven by a keen wind, swirled by, falling endlessly out of a cold, pale sky.

'Mr Decker, I *have* walked in and I *am*

ready to close this station if I don't get your full cooperation,' he said.

Harry Decker, the manager of Radio Beacon, took off his glasses and held them up to catch the light against the lens. Satisfied, he wiped a smear away with a crumpled tissue.

'Look, Markfield, I'm not a fool. Nor am I naive enough to be consoled by a quick — *I'm doing this for your own good!*' Decker leaned forward across his desk. 'At least tell me what's going on. The trouble in Shepthorne may have been a plane crash initially — but it's gone further than that now.'

Markfield turned away from the window and sat down facing Decker and the silent man called Jerry Chapman; Chapman had been the studio-link in contact with Mike Sandler.

'A straightforward air disaster,' Decker went on, 'would normally warrant immediate attention by emergency services. Fire. Police. Ambulance. I might even accept the army in a rescue role. But not as an authoritarian force. Armed and obviously capable of using extreme measures.' He paused again. 'Am I still making sense?'

Markfield's expression remained static. 'It's your story.'

'We have a crashed aircraft. Military. American. Where are the air-crash enquiry people? Isn't it usual for them to be given first look? And what about US Airforce personnel — why aren't they involved? You do see what I'm getting at, Markfield? Too many questions but no answers. Why all the secrecy? What's on that plane that needs to be kept hidden away?'

'I could say you were making too much of a noise about nothing,' Markfield pointed out.

Decker allowed himself a slow smile. 'I don't think you'll do that.'

'Oh? Why?'

'Because there's no way you can effectively wipe out what I know, or what Jerry and Mike Sandler know. Or whoever else might have heard Mike's tape. Granted you could shut the station down. But the knowledge would still be there — in our heads. And it's an odd thing about the journalistic mind. Give it a few facts, then deny it the rest of the story and it develops a passion for digging. And if you dig long enough and hard enough you usually find something.'

'Is that your way of telling me that you intend pursuing this matter?'

'Unless you can convince me there's a good enough reason for letting it die.'

'You're a hard man, Decker.'

'I'm also a responsible man, Markfield. Sensationalism isn't one of my fetishes. I like a good story — but I also know where to draw the line.'

Markfield glanced at Jerry Chapman. He nodded in agreement with Decker's sentiments.

'We're not all out looking for the scoop of the year,' Chapman said.

'Admit it, Markfield,' Decker said. 'You attempted a cover-up over Shepthorne. It hasn't been absolutely effective. As I see it, we, as a news media, have a legitimate right to report on the incident.'

The office became very quiet.

Decker rolled a pen back and forth beneath his fingers.

Jerry Chapman watched Markfield.

And Markfield reached a decision.

He based his decision on a personal assessment of the two men sitting across from him. It was a calculated risk he was about to undertake, but then Markfield recognised life as a continuous relay of decisions, most of which had positive and negative sides to them. Here and now he was risking a great deal, but, as always, he was willing to accept full responsibility.

'Two years ago the British and US defence departments agreed to collaborate on a programme of experimentation intended to develop a counter to the Soviet germ-warfare capability.'

Decker put down the pen he'd been toying with. 'I thought we had more or less outlawed the production of bacteriological weapons?'

'That's true. But while Western governments held back the Russians carried on. At this moment in time the Russian capability is extremely high. They even have organised regiments of troops who are engaged in nothing else but germ-warfare. Their ability to deliver the goods is second to none. They're geared for this kind of activity to the last nut and bolt. Special decontamination units. Their troops provided with protective clothing. If I told you how we are equipped to face this kind of attack you'd have a bloody heart attack. And if anybody thinks the Russians are going to abandon all they've done just because we talk about it being an unethical way of waging war, then he's a damn fool.'

'This British-US cooperation was to create a deterrent weapon?'

Markfield nodded. 'Develop the weapon and *then* let the Russians know about it. Make them see that if they ever threatened to use theirs then retaliation would come from us.'

'A parallel to the nuclear deterrent,' Chapman said.

'Given that the Russians show no intention of destroying *their* stocks of chemical or bacteriological weaponry it left the West in an awkward position.'

'But the development of this British-US weapon was kept secret?' Decker said.

'Public opinion had a lot to do with the

earlier ban on germ-warfare weaponry. The British and the Americans knew that if their plan became public there'd be one hell of an outcry. If the Russians got wind of it they'd have a field day. So the research and development simply maintained a low profile and got on with the job.'

'I'm starting to see a grim picture emerging,' said Decker. 'Along the lines of there being something nasty on board that crashed plane. Something you wish had stayed hidden.'

Markfield smiled awkwardly. Like a schoolboy who had been caught playing a mischievous prank. 'A sample batch of one of the bacteria strains currently under development.'

'I wouldn't have thought flying that sort of stuff back and forth across the Atlantic was the sanest thing to do,' Chapman said grimly.

'Agreed, and up until this flight there were no exchanges of actual bacteria. Everything was done by a special computer-link between the two research establishments. Then a week ago the

American research team had a sudden breakthrough with a strain of the *Yaws* bacteria.'

'*Yaws?*'

'It originated in the African rain forest. It's a spiral bacterium. *Treponema pertenue* by name. Apparently the physical symptoms are similar to syphilis. From what I've learned of the development the new strain is very quick to establish itself and has some ugly side-effects.'

'And they have people actually working to create something like that?' Chapman asked, disbelief in his voice.

'We live in a lousy world,' Markfield said, 'and sometimes it backfires. There was some kind of leak in the American research establishment. Four out of a team of six scientists died and the other two are barely hanging on. The research facility has been isolated because the bacteria has become unstable. The Americans responsible for the development, now dead, had an ongoing dialogue with their British counter-parts — they've been doing work on a neutralising agent, and apparently they're confident of its success. However they needed an actual sample of the new strain in order to carry out final tests. With the bacteria becoming unstable the British team were the only ones capable of coming up with some kind of answer. Which brings us right back to the plane that has unfortunately crashed on Shepthorne.'

'Just how virulent is this unstable bacteria?' Decker asked.

'I'm no scientist,' Markfield pointed out. 'But from what I've been able to deduce the new strain has an accelerated growth rate. The normal reproduction process of bacteria is pretty fast. All bacteria have to do is grow large enough to be able to split into two, the two into four, and so on. This new *Yaws* strain can reproduce within minutes and it has a high resistance to the white blood cells which normally attack any threat of infection to the body.'

'How does this bacteria get into the body?' Chapman asked.

'The *Yaws*-strain is of the contagious

type — simply transmitted by physical contact.'

Chapman glanced at Decker, then back at Markfield. 'Hence the need to isolate Shepthorne?'

'Until a team of specialists arrive from the research establishment we can't — daren't — allow anyone in or out of the village. The sample of bacteria on that plane may have been released. All it would take is for one man or woman to enter that aircraft and touch the capsule containing the bacteria. If the seals had been broken on the capsule that would be it. That one person would become a walking time-bomb. He or she would only have a short time to live, but in that time the bacteria could be passed on to someone else — and so on.'

'If someone *was* infected and managed to leave Shepthorne . . . ?' Decker began.

'You want to know the kind of epidemic we might have to face if an infected person reached some densely populated area?' Markfield shook his head. 'There aren't any calculated forecasts for that, but if the bacteria was carried into a town the result would be, to say the least, devastating. Until it's tested we have no guarantee that the neutralising agent actually works. Even if it is effective it has to be produced in quantity — so it isn't about to be much help to someone who has already picked up the infection and developed the symptoms.'

'If news of this is made public,' Decker said, 'there could be absolute panic.'

'It's inevitable,' Markfield admitted. 'That's what I want to avoid.'

'Let's assume you recover this sample without infection risk. What happens afterwards? Do you still keep quiet about what really happened? Or will you release the story?'

'You don't miss a trick, Decker. Obviously the British and US governments would prefer to keep the whole thing under wraps. A psychological advantage would be gained if we could go to the Russians and say look, your edge in the germ-warfare stakes has been lost because we now have an extremely effective counter-weapon.' He saw the expression on Decker's face. 'Germ-warfare is a dirty business,

Decker. I don't favour the concept personally. But I am aware of the reality of the situation. Like it or not, until we can work out a way of existing without killing each other we have to have the means of defending ourselves. There are a hell of a lot of moral reasons why we *shouldn't* use germ-warfare weaponry. But you can apply that criteria to any and all methods of destruction. What's the alternative? It's fine to say we won't get involved in this or that — and in the meantime your potential enemy is arming himself with everything he can think of. Fine ideals aren't going to be much help come the day that enemy is on your doorstep, backed up by *his* arsenal. What do you do then?'

'Does it justify the stuff on that plane?' Chapman demanded.

'My job doesn't include having to justify a damn thing. I leave that to people who are better qualified.'

'It's a hell of a philosophy,' Chapman mumbled.

'I don't deny it's difficult,' said Markfield. 'Right now, though, all I'm concerned with is the removal of that bacteria from

Shepthorne. And I want it done with the minimum of fuss and the maximum speed.'

Decker glanced at Chapman. 'Well, Stanley, another fine mess you've got me into!'

EFFECT

1

Gas, leaking from a fractured main-pipe, had created a concentrated pocket that lay in the cavities beneath two of the partially demolished buildings at the end of the village street in the vicinity of the old stone bridge. Falling snow had been driven by the gusting wind and had formed thick drifts over and across the shattered remains of the buildings. The fires started by the initial combination of crashing plane and exploding petrol tanks had died down. Here and there tiny pockets of flame lingered, dull embers glowing fitfully in some sheltered corner.

High up on a still-standing section of inner wall, the shredded ends of floor beams, charred black, began to smoulder as eddies of the cold wind curved in through the exposed shell of the building. Fanning the beam ends the stream of air drew out the dormant heat. The wood glowed, smoke whipped away by the wind. Once — twice — it burst into flame, then sputtered out. But the wind persisted, provoking the glowing embers until the flame returned, strengthened, and took hold. Encouraged by the wind the flames grew, biting deep into the wood.

Thick snow, bearing heavily down on the remains of the roof, finally became too much for the weakened section. It began to sag. Slowly at first, drawing down more collected snow from further up. As this concentrated itself on the extreme edge the roof section collapsed with an agonised slowness. Wooden spars and thick roof slates dropped. One main support beam curved down in a pendulum arc that terminated against the remaining section of inner wall. The loosened brickwork came apart in a shower of red dust. A length of blazing floor beam fell, trailing a brilliant tail of hissing sparks in its wake. It struck the debris at floor level, rolling, twisting, then vanished from sight in the dark cavity below.

The resultant explosion — as the

trapped gas below the building ignited — concentrated its force in a vertical direction. The first explosion triggered a second, and two buildings vanished in a concentrated blast of released energy. Flame and smoke lashed skywards. More found escape at ground level, scorching a terrible path of destruction along the already ravaged village street . . .

★ ★ ★

Two of Peter Mather's men, part of the guard around the crashed Hercules, were close enough to the blast to be fatally involved. They stood no chance as the raw power of the explosion reached out with searing fingers, plucking them off the ground and hurling them into eternity. Their blackened, shrivelled bodies were thrown twenty yards along the street.

The remaining men guarding the plane were knocked about by the heavy shock waves and battered by flying debris.

As one soldier clambered slowly to his feet, groping for the weapon he'd dropped, he became aware of a huge black shadow moving to engulf him. Still only half-risen he glanced skywards, and saw the huge tail section of the Hercules swinging lazily round as the plane was moved by the force of the explosion. The soldier closed his fingers over the rifle and began to rise to his feet. He could hear a soft creaking sound, accompanied by the harsher screech of protesting metal as it weakened and gave under tremendous pressure . . . and then it was too late . . . the rear fuselage of the Hercules dropped, a dead weight coming to ground, and the impact crushed the soldier against the hard earth, splintering his bones and reducing his flesh to a red smear.

Sergeant Duggan leapt out of the command helicopter and ran in the direction of the Hercules. He could see staggering figures emerging from the swirl of smoke and dust and driving snow. Reaching the first one he took the man's arm and directed him away from the vicinity of the plane.

'You hurt, Evans?' he yelled above the noise.

The young soldier stared at him through the streaked visor of his hood. His eyes were wide and round with shock.

'Get over there by the chopper,' Duggan ordered, giving the man a shove.

Nearing the plane Duggan saw another suited figure rising from its knees. A glistening mass of red marked the sleeve of the soldier's protective suit and he was making a vain attempt at stopping the flow of bright blood from spurting through his fingers.

'Stand still, you silly bugger!' Duggan said. He opened the pouch of field-dressings clipped to his belt and took out a pressure-pad. Knocking aside the soldier's bloody fingers Duggan calmly placed the pad over the deep, pulpy wound. Then he firmly placed the man's hand over the dressing. 'Now keep it there! And walk . . . I mean *walk* . . . over to the chopper. Captain Mather will get the doc to see to you.'

Duggan moved on. He kept well clear of the Hercules, even though he was sure the thing wouldn't move again. He was more concerned about his men. He eyed the billowing flames rising from the remains of the buildings where the explosion had occurred, and wondered what else could possibly go wrong. He was ready to believe anything. It had been that kind of day right from the start — and it wasn't over yet.

★ ★ ★

They had to get out of the house, Elouise decided. Regardless of what was happening outside — soldiers and all — they couldn't stay where they were.

The abrupt and terrifying explosion had dislodged masses of debris that had crashed down around them. Elouise had covered Allison's body with her own, and by some miracle nothing more dangerous than a few odd lumps of broken brickwork had hit them. Even so they were covered in choking dust.

One more explosion like that, Elouise decided, and the whole house would come down around their ears! Next time they probably wouldn't escape so lightly.

'Come along, dear,' she said gently, and

pulled Allison to her feet.

'Are we going for a walk?' Alison asked; her voice had taken on a chilling innocence that was childlike; she gazed at Elouise through vacant eyes; her mouth was held partially open, lips slack. 'That will be nice. A walk in the snow.'

Elouise could have wept. She hoped that Allison's condition was no more than a state of shock brought about by her injuries, the loss of blood and her exposure to the cold.

'Yes, we're going to go for a walk,' she said.

She led Allison through the shattered house, guiding her over piles of rubble. The remnants of their life scattered all around. In the shadowed ruins of the hall Elouise struggled to open a cupboard door, pushing aside a heap of splintered planking from the collapsed ceiling. Ignoring cut fingers and scraped skin she eventually managed to clear the door. From the cupboard she took thick coats and wellington boots, scarves and gloves. Putting on her own Elouise helped her sister to dress. Allison needed telling before she would make any attempt herself; again there was the childlike dependence on someone taking the responsibility from her.

When they were suitably dressed Elouise led Allison from the house. They clambered awkwardly over heaped rubble, covered by thick snow. Standing finally on the street Elouise glanced along the length of the ruined village. She found difficulty in accepting what she saw at first. The beautiful place that had become home to her and Allison lay in ruins. Destroyed. Practically levelled to the ground. Flames curling up from piles of rubble that had once been homes and shops; where people she knew had lived and worked. My God, where were they all? How many were dead? Or trapped under piles of fallen masonry? Hurt and in pain! For the first time since the whole nightmare had commenced Elouise felt tears fill her eyes. She began to cry, and it was as much for the death of Shepthorne itself as it was for the people who lived there.

'I'm cold!' Allison's petulant complaint cut through Elouise's moment of sorrow.

'Elouise, I'm very, very cold!'

'Oh, yes, dear,' Elouise said. 'Let's carry on and see if we meet anyone we know.'

They stumbled along the middle of the road. Elouise averted her eyes as they reached the line of burned-out vehicles and their black, skeletal occupants; Allison appeared not to have noticed; she was conducting some private conversation with herself about some episode from her childhood.

Once or twice Elouise became aware of the shadowy figures of the armed soldiers moving about. The bulky suits and visored hoods gave them a sinister aspect. They took note of the two sisters as they passed, but made no attempt at contact. Elouise decided not to become too inquisitive.

As they neared the far end of the street Elouise spotted a tall figure coming towards them. As the figure took on shape and substance Elouise felt a surge of relief.

'Oh, Major Dolby, I'm so pleased to see you!' she said, and urged Allison forward as the major raised a hand in recognition.

* * *

'You're going to leave me! Damn you, Sam, I can tell when you're lying!'

'Of course I'm not going to leave you,' Sam snapped; his anger came from being caught out. He *was* going to leave her. He knew it and so did Dawn. 'I can't get you free from under that lot. I need help. That's what I'm going for.'

'You bastard! You selfish, ungrateful bastard!' Dawn let her head fall back. The effort of holding it up so that she could see him proved too much for her. She was getting weaker with every passing minute. Though she wasn't aware of it blood was seeping from her crushed leg in a continuous stream. Already her face had taken on a translucent pallor. She was having difficulty keeping her eyes open. She was dying. Slowly. But very surely.

'There are people down there in the street,' Sam said. 'It won't take me long to get a few of them up here. They probably have the equipment we need to lift that heavy stuff off you.'

He stood up and began to edge away from her, waiting for the moment when her concentration drifted again. He saw her eyes begin to droop. To close. Now! Now, you stupid sod, get the hell out of here! He turned and stumbled, catching his foot on some loose bricks. The noise filled the room.

'Sam? Oh, Sam, where are you?' Dawn's voice failed to rise above a frantic, pleading whisper. 'Please stay with me, Sam, I'm so scared! Sam! Sam . . . please don't . . . leave . . . me . . . '

He was through the sagging doorway. Emerging on the landing. Ahead of him lay the oak stairs that led down to the reception area. Sam found the stairs littered with fallen debris. White drifts of snow lay over piles of rubble. He glanced up and saw a section of pale sky gleaming through the gaping roof. Halfway down the stairs he was forced to climb over a mass of rubble. As he eased his way down the far side the whole stair structure began to move sideways. Sam froze. He could hear the wood of the stair creaking and groaning all around him. Sweat beaded his face. He let his weight down on one foot. Bricks and plaster gave way under him. Sam groaned as he felt himself slide. He clawed at the rubble but it simply crumbled beneath his fingers. He slithered helplessly down the stairs, a heavy shower of debris following him, half covering his body. He came to a stop against the bottom rail of the stair, still able to feel the whole structure swaying and settling beneath him. He pulled his body out from under the rubble and stood up very slowly. Holding on tightly to the rail he descended to the foot of the stairs.

At the bottom he saw a body partly buried. The head had been badly crushed by some heavy object and was covered in dark, dried blood. A raw mass bulged out of the split skull. There was enough of the face left for Sam to be able to recognise the landlord of the Shepthorne Arms Hotel.

Sam made his way across the lobby. A mass of rubble effectively blocked off the main door. He hesitated. Turning, he recrossed the lobby, pushing his way through an oak door that led into the small Residents Bar. There was a window that opened on to the street. He could get out through that.

He glanced around the room. It barely resembled the intimate, cosy place where he and Dawn had spent long evenings sitting before an open fire in the big stone hearth. The room was thick with dust now. Half the ceiling had fallen in, and the polished oak bar had collapsed under the weight of a huge beam that had dropped across it. Sam did notice one or two bottles still standing on the shelf at the back of the bar. He stared at them for a while. A quick smile touched his lips. A drink would be very welcome, he decided. He was feeling bloody dry. And who was going to say anything to stop him?

Sam clambered over the bar, glass crunching under his shoes. He picked up a bottle of expensive whisky and blew off the dust. He nodded in approval when he saw that it was almost full. He unscrewed the cap and put the bottle to his lips. The whisky tasted good. Sam took a long swallow, allowing the mellow liquid to slide slowly down his throat.

He sat down with his back to the wall. Now he had time to think. To plan his next moves. His main objective was to get away from the village. Make his way back to London and then to his flat in Kensington. If he could reach the flat he was home safe. A change of clothes and a little doctoring would get his appearance back to normal. Of course he was going to have to do some fast thinking to explain why he'd failed to attend the meeting. But that was the least of his worries. He took another long swallow from the bottle. Had he forgotten anything? There was nothing up in the room to identify him. He'd learned long ago how to conduct his illicit weekends. He never carried any personal identification. Just a wallet containing cash. No cheques or credit cards. A false name for the register. A small travelling case holding nightwear, disposable shaving gear. Cheap stuff he bought just for the occasion. He always travelled in the same way, by train and then taxi. Paying with cash. Careful. Discreet. Avoiding anything that might attract attention. And it worked. It had worked for a long time. No one had ever suspected. Least of all his wife. She was content anyway with the big house down in Esher. Her own little world of social gatherings. Her friends. The children. If Sam rang and said he was staying over in town for the weekend she never suspected he was involved in anything other than the business meetings he invented. Delia's mind didn't work that way. Sam wished he could say the same for the members of his board. Maybe it was the business they were in that made them naturally suspicious. Nothing but a bunch of old women! It didn't make Sam's life any easier.

★ ★ ★

Smithy had reached the street. He stood mutely surveying the increasing activity. He was beyond really caring what it was all about. Smithy simply wanted help.

151

Someone able to give him relief from the pain. He didn't care how they did it as long as . . . Through hideously swollen eyes he caught a blurred image of his own bloated hands. The discoloured flesh was cratered with oozing, bloody sores; the change from healthy tissue to decay seemed to be accelerating; the pain had increased too, deep rooted now, making his very bones ache, and Smithy had noticed an increasing stiffness in his joints.

He shuffled forward, out across the street, and saw a group of figures a few yards to his left. Smithy turned towards them. Maybe they could help him. He beckoned with his hands. The group remained motionless, faces nothing more than pale blurs.

'Don't go near him!' a man's voice commanded.

Then a woman: 'He's funny!'

A second female voice. This one full of concern. Alarmed. 'Allison, come back! Allison! Allis . . . Don't! Don't!'

Smithy felt gentle hands touch his. The contact alarmed him. He remembered the man in the house; the way he'd drawn back from Smithy's touch — the look on his face.

A mêlée of voices erupted. All shouting. Yelling. Arguing. Smithy fell back. Fear rose in his mind. There was much to be frightened of. So many things to threaten him. In his confusion he failed to understand that the bacteria destroying his body was doing the same to his mind — creating false terrors. Implanting doubt where there was nothing to fear.

He turned and began to run. He had no destination. No intent. He was simply running to escape from some unknown threat, and in doing so he unwittingly ran directly at another.

Again more shouting. This time ahead of him. Smithy stumbled. His feet went from under him and he smashed to the ground. Sobbing he dragged himself upright.

He sensed movement before him. He lifted his head, peering through the tears filling his eyes. Dark, moving figures closed in on him.

Smithy stood still. He was trapped.

They wanted to cage him in.

But he wouldn't let them!

A harsh voice boomed at him.

A thunderous roar of noise filled Smithy's ears.

He waved his arms at the dim figures. All he wanted to do was to make them go away. But the figures refused. They shimmered before his dulling vision. Smithy lunged forward in an attempt to brush past them.

Something struck him in the chest. A terrible pain spread across his body. It grew and filled his whole being. A numbness came over him. He wasn't even aware of falling, of hitting the ground. He lay staring up at the pale sky. Soft snowflakes settled on the ravaged skin of his face. They felt briefly cooling. Smithy choked as warm fluid filled his throat. He began to cough. More of the fluid rose, spraying from his mouth. A trembling spasm shook him. Smithy kicked in a final reflex action, his body reacting to the bullet that had torn through his chest. He died in silent agony, not even aware that he'd been shot.

'That's right, Markfield, it's already happened. Some poor sod has already come into contact with the stuff!'

'What have you done about it?'

Peter Mather stared at the radio as if it were Markfield himself. He swore under his breath before speaking into the handset. 'I'll tell you what we've done, Markfield. We've shot the bastard! What else was there to do? He was beyond any kind of help.'

'Did he come into contact with anyone else?'

'One woman we know of. How many others there's no way of telling. Look, Markfield, I don't think this is going to work. Maybe we can stop people from entering or leaving Shepthorne, but we can't guarantee others won't be infected. There are too many people unaccounted for. We've no way of knowing how many are trapped under collapsed homes. This place is a complete shambles. People wandering about. I've got the local police raising all kinds of hell because I refuse to let them help. It's bad enough without this damned bacteria being passed around. And what happens if people do start dying all over the place? We can't do much about moving them if this bloody germ doesn't die along with them. How do we get rid of it?'

Markfield hesitated, but only for a moment. 'Burn them!'

'What?'

'Any bodies with the bacteria symptoms,' Markfield repeated. 'Just burn them! I don't care who protests. Destroy the bodies with fire. It's all that's left open to us.'

'Us?' Mather said. 'I'm looking around, Markfield, but I don't see you here with me.'

There was a weary sigh on the other end of the radio-link. 'We'll argue the point later, Captain. For now just follow your orders.'

'All right, Markfield. But for Christ's sake get those bloody white-coated wonders down here fast! The way things are going we'll all end up like that poor bugger one of my men had to shoot. If you could see what he looks like maybe you'd realise why I'm getting worried.'

Mather dropped the handset and climbed out of the command helicopter. Sergeant Duggan was standing just beside the open door. He glanced at Mather.

'Did I hear him right, sir?' he asked. 'About burning bodies?'

Mather nodded. It was a thought that refused to sit lightly with him. 'Our man from the ministry has given us the word, and we are required to carry it out to the letter.'

'Bloody liberty,' Duggan muttered. 'What are we supposed to do about that woman who touched that bloke? Do we shoot *her* if she starts to go the way he did?'

'That, Sergeant, is a very good question.'

Mather fell in beside his sergeant as they began the long trek through the village to where his men were holding Vivian Dolby and Elouise Smythe. He was going to have to talk to them. Try to reason with them. But how did he tell the woman that her sister was going to die?

And they were all going to have to stand back and allow it to happen without lifting a finger.

★ ★ ★

'Harrison, what's going on up there?' Jenny asked. 'That was a gunshot a little while ago wasn't it?'

He nodded.

'And that explosion. What caused that?'

'Maybe escaping gas in one of the houses.'

Jenny shuddered. 'It's all like some terrible bad dream.'

'Hey,' he said. 'You quit talking like that.'

'Can I change the subject?'

'Sure.'

'I don't want to be a bore — but I'm awfully cold.' He took off the thick sheepskin coat and leaned into the car to wrap it round her upper body. Jenny couldn't help noticing how blue his bruised and bloody hands were. Her self-pity evaporated. Tears misted her eyes. God, how could she worry about herself when he was struggling to help her and probably suffering himself.

'Oh, Harrison, I'm sorry,' she said.

'What for?'

'Grumbling about being cold. Just look at your hands!'

'I can always type with my toes,' he grinned. 'Now shut up and keep your fingers crossed. I'm going to try again.'

He leaned inside the car, his shoulder pressing against Jenny's knees as he sank his arms in the cold water filling the lower half of the compartment. He couldn't see where Jenny's left ankle was caught. He was forced to operate by feel, trying to wedge the tyre-lever between the clutch and the bulkhead so that he could obtain enough pressure to force the clutch to one side. His first attempts had failed because the lever had slipped the moment he'd applied pressure. And he had to be careful not to catch the lever against Jenny's ankle. She hadn't made any fuss but he knew the operation must have been causing her considerable pain. He realised too that having her legs submerged in the freezing water for such a long period could lead to problems. The cold water was making it difficult for him. After a couple of minutes his fingers became numb and he had difficulty controlling his actions. Once he'd dropped the lever and it took long minutes before he located it.

'Hold on,' he said. 'I think I've got the lever in place.'

Harrison braced himself against the sill of the Triumph. He closed his raw fingers tightly around the lever beneath the water and took a long, deep breath.

'If you feel the clutch move try and pull your foot out.'

'I'm ready.'

'Now!'

He drew back on the lever. There was no immediate movement. After a few seconds he felt sure that the lever was drawing the clutch away from Jenny's ankle.

'I think it's moving!' Jenny said excitedly.

Even as she spoke the lever slipped. The Triumph rocked. Without warning it began to slide, the rear swinging round towards the water. Jenny screamed. She made a grab for Harrison as he threw his arms around her. He refused to let go of her even as the Triumph turned sideways on and went over the edge of the bank and into the River Shep.

* * *

Crouched in the shadows beneath a tangled mass of splintered wood Eddie Frame watched the armed soldiers moving back and forth along the village street. He'd seen them shoot the pitiful figure of the man who had burst in on Eddie and his dead wife. Eddie couldn't forget the man's face. Covered in festering, oozing sores. The eyes almost lost in swollen rolls of flesh. The bloated, cracked lips bleeding and running with thick saliva. And the clawing hands that had reached out to touch him, the skin hanging from the tips. Eddie had almost been sick when he'd felt one of those hands touch him. Scaly fingers running lightly across the back of his left hand.

He absently scratched at an itchy spot

on that hand as he eyed the soldiers in their bulky suits. They looked like aliens from some TV film. But this was no make-believe movie. This was happening for real. He glanced at the body of the man who had been shot. He wouldn't get up and go home when it was all over. Not the way they did in the films. But the way they were shot in the films didn't resemble the real thing at all. Eddie had never seen anyone shot before. It was an experience he didn't want repeated. Christ, it had been terrible. The way that bullet had blasted a raw hole right through the writhing body. Blood and flesh spouting out in an obscene spray. And the way the poor beggar had squirmed and wriggled about on the ground, his arms and legs jerking . . .

Eddie scratched at his hand again. The irritation was getting worse. He felt other itchy spots break out. On his shoulders. Down his back . . . a particularly nasty one on his neck, just below his jaw. And then he began to feel sick. His stomach churned and a nauseous sensation flooded his throat. He felt so bad he let himself sag back against a solid wedge of timber. Eddie closed his eyes and remained perfectly still, hoping that the sickness would go away. It was probably reaction setting in. After all that had happened today he could expect it. But the sickness stayed, and got worse. He felt hot. Then cold. Sweat rolled greasily down his face. Eddie began to heave. His stomach lurched wildly, muscles tightening and relaxing. Dizziness swept over him and Eddie lost his balance. Even though he was sitting down he couldn't control himself and he rolled over on to his side. A rush of vomit filled his throat and burst from his lips. He lay curled up, his body humping in pain, the spasms continuing long after there was nothing left to evacuate from his stomach.

Some time later he sat up, moaning softly. His body ached. Worse though, the entire surface of his skin itched and crawled with some irritation that gave him the feeling of being covered with thousands of tiny, living insects. Eddie began to rub his face, his hands, and his body through his clothing. The irritation became unbearable. He scrambled from his place of concealment and ran out into the street. As he ran he began to tear at his clothing. He had to get at his itching skin. Somehow he had to wipe away all those wriggling, creeping, crawling things that were covering him.

★　★　★

The bottle of whisky had not had the effect Sam Mayhew required. Under normal circumstances a few glasses of whisky calmed him down and brought on a feeling of contentment and well-being. Today all he'd received was a headache. He decided it was time to leave Shepthorne. Tossing aside the bottle he had made his way to the window, eased it open, and climbed carefully over the sill. There were a couple of cars parked close to the front of the hotel and Sam got down behind one of them to survey the layout of the street.

If he could make it to the other side of the street and take cover behind one of the abandoned, burned-out vehicles there, he might be able to work his way down to the river's edge and then along the bank to some spot where he could cut off across country.

He glanced up at the sky. The snow showed no sign of slacking off. That was good. The falling snow would help to conceal his movements.

Sam turned up the collar of his jacket. Pity he hadn't brought a topcoat with him to Shepthorne. Stop moaning, he told himself. You can put up with a bit of cold!

He moved to the rear of the car, edging out slowly. The street seemed fairly quiet. Sam stood up and cut off across the street.

He failed to see the running figure loom out of the snow. There was a rush of sound. Sam glanced over his shoulder and saw a wide-eyed figure almost upon him. The man was pulling at his clothing with oddly swollen hands. There was only time for a quick glimpse of the distorted features as Sam tried to step aside.

The man collided with Sam. For a few seconds of disorientation the two men remained locked in a tangle of arms and hands. Then they separated. Sam continued on across the street, rounding the bonnet of a burned-out van. He dropped to his knees, crouching tightly against one of the front wheels.

Nothing happened for a couple of long minutes. Nodding to himself Sam wriggled on his stomach over the grass verge and down the long slope to the river's edge. He reached it without being challenged. Again he paused, lying for a long time in the cold snow as he explored the possibilities open to him. His best way seemed to be the spot where the road curved round to enter the village. The road itself was blocked by burned-out vehicles, but there was plenty of concealment offered by the thick grass and undergrowth that lay below the wall, edging the road and forming a narrow bank for the river as it curved round to run parallel with the road. If he could get as far as there nothing was going to stop him.

★   ★   ★

'But I can't just leave her lying there!' Elouise protested. 'She is my sister

— don't you understand?' She turned to Vivian Dolby in a silent appeal for support.

'Miss Smythe — Elouise — I'm sure the captain appreciates your concern. We all do, my dear, but as hard as it may seem I think we *must* do as he asks.' Dolby sensed Elouise's vulnerability. He put an arm around her shoulder.

'Thank you, Major,' Peter Mather said. He took a couple of unobtrusive steps to the side, beckoning to Sergeant Duggan. 'Have one of the men stay close to that infected woman. See to it that no one touches her. And bring me Inspector Henderson.'

Duggan nodded and strode away.

Alone for a moment Mather glanced at his watch. How much longer before those damn scientists arrived? Mather was beginning to count the odds, and they appeared to be getting shorter all the time.

A commotion further up the street attracted his attention. Mather snatched his pistol from the holster on his belt.

He saw a lurching figure materialise out

of the snowmist. Mather felt his stomach tighten as he caught a glimpse of the man's face.

Another one! Not yet as advanced as the first but already showing a reaction to the infection.

Beyond the advancing man Mather thought he saw a second figure. It was hard to be certain as the falling snow tended to break up solid shapes; made them almost shadowy — insubstantial against the drifting backdrop.

'You . . . ' Mather challenged. 'Stay where you are!'

The man hesitated, staring at Mather through glazed eyes. For a moment Mather imagined the man to be doing as he'd ordered. But the figure lurched forward, seeming to cast aside his initial hesitation.

Close up the man's face showed clearly the extent of the infection: red blotches marking the skin; the swelling, puffy blisters already far advanced.

'Do as I say and we'll try and help you,' Mather said. 'I don't want to have to use this.' He levelled the automatic pistol.

The man halted. He stood motionless, eyes staring wildly about him. Mather could see the fear in them. And he could hear the breath rasping from the swollen throat.

So what the hell do I do now? Mather's eye was drawn to the barrel of his pistol; it was quivering visibly. So, I'm good and scared. Well, damnit, why shouldn't I be? Stuck here in the middle of this half-demolished village. Surrounded by fire and snow and corpses, and now a man-made, runaway disease nobody has a proper cure for! How many more are going to be infected before they stop it? If it can be stopped . . .

The infected man uttered a low moan. Whether prompted by pain or anger it heralded an unexpected and violent reaction.

Lunging forward the man ran directly at Mather. There was little chance of avoiding the headlong rush. The man's hands were outstretched and they struck Mather on the shoulders, driving him back. His boots slipped on the hard-packed snow and he slid down on one

169

knee. Mather swung the pistol up at the man's body, and as the straining form fell across him, Mather pulled the trigger. He fired three times, each shot tearing its way through flesh and bone and muscle . . .

★ ★ ★

'There's no way you can keep it secret now,' Decker said.

Markfield didn't look at him. He was deep in thought, as he had been ever since his conversation with Peter Mather.

'You can't silence a whole bloody village,' Decker went on, determined now to force his argument. 'Not in this country anyway.'

'What do you want, Decker?' Markfield snapped. 'My go-ahead for you to slip it into the mid-afternoon news?'

Jerry Chapman sighed. He half rose from his seat and Decker had to wave him back.

'You know I wouldn't even think along those lines,' Decker said.

Markfield gazed at him. He let his rigid shoulders sag and flopped into a chair.

'You're right, of course. We have failed to carry out our original intention.'

'Only in one respect,' Chapman said. 'Surely the most important consideration is the containment of the infection within the area your people have sealed off?'

Markfield grimaced. 'Providing we *can* contain it!'

★   ★   ★

Peering through the streaming window of the helicopter Martin Cooper tried to pick out some kind of identifiable landmark; all he *could* see was a swirling white fog of snow.

'Trust the Yanks,' he muttered. 'They might at least have chosen a decent day to crash.'

His companion, Simon Webb, a tall, lean young man who somehow managed to always appear totally removed from any crisis occurring around or near him, fiddled impatiently with the facepiece of his protective suit's headgear.

'We should be arriving in a few minutes,' he said.

Martin grinned. 'That's what they've been telling us for the last couple of hours. Trouble is they couldn't get that information through to whoever's controlling the weather.'

Even as he spoke the helicopter began to descend, sinking rapidly groundwards.

'Look!' Simon pointed through the window.

Below they could see the whole of Shepthorne — the dark scar left by the crippled aircraft as it had made its destructive landing. Despite the misty curtain of drifting snow they were able to make out the shattered remains of buildings, flames rising here and there amid coils of thick smoke that were whipped away by the wind. They saw, too, the moving figures — the precise, controlled actions of the uniformed men ringing the area — and within the contained village the unsteady, disorientated, stumbling figures of the occupants of the village as they began to drift out from the ruined shells of their former homes.

'They've had it rough,' Simon said.

'Not as rough as it'll get if we can't deal with that damn bacteria,' Martin remarked coldly.

The helicopter swung across to the far side of the disaster area, angling down in a sharp descent that brought it to earth only yards from the army command helicopter.

As Simon slid open the door, flinching against the cold blast of wind and driven snow, a running figure approached the helicopter.

'Doctor Cooper?'

'No. I'm Webb. Doctor Cooper's inside. We're supposed to contact a Captain Mather.'

'That isn't going to be possible, Doctor,' Sergeant Duggan said.

'What's happened?'

'The captain's been infected.'

'You mean the bacteria strain is exposed?' Martin Cooper had picked up the conversation as he had clambered out of the helicopter, dragging a couple of metal containers with him. 'How many have been infected?'

'Four that we can account for. Two are

dead. There's a woman in a bad way — and now Captain Mather,' Duggan concluded bitterly.

'Damn!' Martin said.

'Didn't you know the stuff had been released?' Duggan asked.

'No we *did* not!' Simon said sharply. He yelled to the pilot of the helicopter to make contact with Kevin Markfield. It took a few minutes before Markfield's flat tones came over the headset Simon had put on. 'Markfield? This is Simon Webb. Just explain your bloody silly game to me!'

'I'm not sure I understand, Doctor Webb,' Markfield's voice soothed.

'You're a liar, Markfield. Why didn't you tell us the bacteria has already contaminated a number of people?'

'Until you arrived in Shepthorne it wouldn't have served any purpose to let you know. However, now that you have discovered it — and it's only one small outbreak — I suggest you proceed with your operation as quickly as possible.' There was a soft click as Markfield broke radio contact.

Simon climbed out of the helicopter and raised his face skywards, allowing cold snowflakes to settle on his flesh.

'Well?' Martin asked.

'He didn't tell us because he decided it wasn't necessary!'

Martin's face clouded with anger. 'I imagine it's more to do with trying to keep quiet about the whole bloody mess.'

'Look,' Duggan interrupted. 'I'd like to know where I stand. With Captain Mather out of action I'm automatically in command until I hear otherwise. Do you want me to maintain the situation?'

Martin nodded. 'Overall responsibility is Markfield's. But here and now we're the ones who have to make the choices. The main thing is to keep this area isolated, Sergeant. Carry on as before. Make certain all your men are aware of the contagion. Remember that this bacteria is unstable. We can't be fully certain of any side-effects that might crop up. We do know that its transference is virtually instantaneous, so make your men realise they can't afford any mistakes!'

'How long is it going to take to get that stuff sealed off?'

The two scientists exchanged glances.

'Difficult to estimate,' Simon declared. 'No one's set a precedent for a situation like this, so we take it one step at a time.'

Duggan nodded. 'Very well, sir, I'll try and keep the situation under control.'

'Do I detect a note of doubt?' Simon asked.

'I'm worried about any further infection. If this disease can spread as easily as you suggest we could be in for trouble.'

'I wish we could offer you some kind of guarantee it won't happen,' Martin said. 'The problem is we won't be able to develop any kind of anti-bacteria until we get this sample into the lab and under test.'

Duggan moved away to issue orders to his men, leaving the two scientists alone to gaze up at the snow-shrouded hulk of the aircraft.

'Ready?' Martin said.

Simon closed the visor on his hood, turned and picked up one of the metal containers. Following suit, Martin fell in beside his companion and they tramped awkwardly towards the plane.

Standing beneath the curving fuselage they searched for a way in. It was Simon who eventually discovered the open hatch on the far side of the aircraft — the hatch the man called Smithy had used. Pushing the containers ahead of them the two scientists dragged themselves inside the fuselage . . .

* * *

The snow continued falling. The driving wind pushed it into soft drifts that piled against any object in its path. The wind also encouraged fires to keep burning, fanning the flames.

The last building at the far end of the street, closest to the aircraft, had housed an ironmongery business. Now, shop and living accommodation lay in ruins; somewhere beneath the piles of debris lay the bodies of the man and woman who had owned and run the shop. Badly damaged by the aircraft the building had been further destroyed in the gas explosion and subsequent blaze.

Flames had been working steadily at the wooden floor of the shop for some time. Gradually the intensity of the fire increased until eager flames were licking up the sides of the splintered counter-unit. Once the flames reached the height of the counter, the wind, slicing in through the shattered shop frontage, caught and held them. The fire took hold then, and anything combustible was added to the blaze. Thick smoke rose from the depths of the building. The buffeting wind snatched up glowing embers and tossed them into the air; it lifted them out of the hollow shell of the building, carrying them as if they were no more than leaves tumbling from autumn trees. And then, with the same casual ease, it dropped them. The glowing embers spun to earth, still flickering, trailing bright sparks.

Many of them sank into deep snow, dying in a soft trail of smoke and steam. Others landed on scattered debris, lingered, then faded.

A few drifted down to enter the

hovering fumes rising from the gallons of aviation fuel still spilling from the ruptured wing tanks of the Hercules.

The resultant flash of igniting fuel engulfed the mid and rear section of the aircraft. Brilliant balls of flame smothered the fuselage, rocking the huge frame of the plane. It buckled aluminium panels and probed with hungry, searing fingers, deep inside the cavernous interior of the cargo area . . .

★   ★   ★

'Couldn't you have told me?' Inspector Henderson asked. 'Good God, man, we might have avoided this very thing.'

Peter Mather shook his head slowly. It hurt too much to make any quick movements. His whole body hurt. It was like some deep-rooted ache. A terrible sensation that nagged at every nerve end. It was coupled with a powerful sickness, a wretched nausea that kept him on the brink of vomiting every few seconds; only there was nothing left to bring up. He'd been racked by powerful retching spasms until his stomach was dry, empty. All he could do now was sit huddled in a blanket, his back against the wheel of an abandoned truck. Beneath the blanket he scratched endlessly at the raw, festering flesh of his hands; they were covered in masses of ugly sores, as was his face and body — and he knew that there was nothing anyone could do for him. He was going to die. Most probably in agony. He wasn't sure just when. But the outcome was inevitable.

'I had my orders, Inspector,' he said slowly; it was becoming more and more difficult for him to talk. 'We couldn't risk allowing anyone in or out of the village until we knew the bacteria was secure.'

'Damn you people and your bloody security!' Henderson said. 'If you put as much effort and ingenuity into making peace as you do perpetuating war, I think we'd all be better off!'

'Do what you can with the people available,' Mather said. 'Round up all the survivors you can find. But be careful of anyone you suspect of having the infection. Remember it only needs the slightest physical contact.'

'Is there anything I can do for you?'

'I won't be able to shake this off with a couple of aspirins. Don't worry about me, Inspector, just concentrate on those worth saving.'

Henderson crossed the road to where a tiny group of huddled figures stood. He looked them over. Maybe not his personal choice, but in the circumstances he wasn't going to get any other help.

Major Vivian Dolby and Elouise Smythe. The young man from the radio-car, Mike Sandler. The fourth member of the group was his own Sergeant Manning.

He attracted their attention, and began to speak . . .

At that precise moment the fuel tanks of the downed Hercules exploded in a horrendous burst of livid flame . . .

* * *

With the explosion of the aircraft's fuel tanks the situation became intolerable as far as Larry Kemp was concerned.

Matters appeared to be getting progressively worse.

People being shot. Others running round suffering from some hideous disease. Fire. Death and destruction.

Then Captain Mather himself being struck down by . . . what?

And now another explosion. This time the plane itself.

Kemp had stood it for as long as he could. Now he reached his irreversible decision without any deliberate mental effort. The solution offered itself to him as a definite course of action. He would get away from this place. Just up and walk! Leave his rifle, slip away, and that would end his involvement with the army!

He glanced around. He was pretty well on his own at the moment. All attention was focused on the blazing aircraft. The section he was guarding, close to the fence bordering the road that led into the village, was deserted, having been cleared completely by the troops on their arrival. On the far side of the river, in the village itself, Kemp could see a fair amount of activity. There were quite a few people moving about now as more survivors began to emerge from the ruined buildings. A short while ago another helicopter had arrived, landing in the vicinity of the plane. Now, with the sudden explosion, the plane had become the centre of attraction.

Kemp threw his rifle down. A feeling of relief washed over him; he was glad to be rid of the thing; he hated the weapon and its attendant implications of death and destruction. He turned and made for the fence that would give him access to the road. Climbing it was difficult in the cumbersome, restricting suit. Kemp tore off his thick gloves and began to open the suit's fastenings. He shrugged out of it, unmindful of the sudden chill as the driving wind slapped at him. He zipped up his combat jacket and returned to the fence. It was easier to climb now. Once over it he clambered up the sloping bank and broke through the line of burned-out vehicles. He crossed the road, floundered through deep drifts of snow and climbed the fence on the opposite side. He found himself in a ditch that bordered a wide, sloping field curving off into the misty distance. Kemp grinned to himself. No problem now. All he had to do was keep going. Across the field and straight on to wherever it led him. He glanced up at the sky. The snow looked set to keep coming. He took a quick glance at his watch and saw that it was mid-afternoon. It would get dark soon. They would never find him. Not now. And even if they did catch up with him, and take him back, all he'd get was time in the glasshouse. After that they'd kick him out of the army anyway. So he couldn't lose, no matter what.

He stood up and clambered out of the ditch. He glanced back over his shoulder briefly. Over the tops of the trees he could still see the smoke rising from the burning aircraft. Let the stupid bastards sort that mess out for themselves, he thought, and cut off across the wide, empty, snow-covered field.

$\star$　$\star$　$\star$

Later, much later, they found what was left of Simon Webb's body still inside the gutted wreck of the Hercules.

By some unexplainable circumstance Martin Cooper survived the explosion and the burst of raw flame that filled the interior of the aircraft.

There were two explosions. Both close together and barely noticed by those on the outside. The first was the igniting of the spilled fuel; this concentrated its force on the shell of the fuselage and the already weakened wings of the aircraft; the fuselage split apart under the pressure and it was during the second explosion — of the wing tanks themselves, which resulted in a blast of flaming fuel — that Martin Cooper was caught in the tail end of the shock wave from the initial explosion and hurled bodily from the fuselage. He was thrown clear of the aircraft, his protective suit ablaze with burning fuel. Virtually unconscious, his limp body free from any tension, he smashed into a deep drift of snow, and lay motionless until he was dug free by Sergeant Duggan and two of his men.

They dragged the dazed and groaning scientist clear of the blazing aircraft, and the army doctor wrenched off Martin's hood. There was a nasty bruise on Martin's left cheek and blood trickling from his mouth and nose.

'Is he alive?' Duggan asked.

The doctor was busy checking the scientist's pulse. After a minute he raised his head.

'Alive and about ready to start kicking,' he said.

Duggan breathed a sigh of relief.

There was a convulsive movement from the figure lying on the ground. Martin's eyes suddenly opened wide. He stared around him, peering at the faces watching him.

'Simon! Where's Simon?'

Duggan glanced at the doctor, then across at the blazing aircraft. 'I don't think he made it, Doctor Cooper.'

A low groan came from Martin's lips. He pushed aside the helping hands and sat up, holding his aching head in his hands.

'I hate asking this right now,' Duggan said. 'But did you find the bacteria sample?'

Martin nodded. 'The capsule was there on its cradle. The outer-casing box had been opened. The capsule itself was leaking — probably caused during the crash. We found an old shotgun on the floor of the cargo area, so obviously somebody had been inside. Whoever it was must have opened the box and touched the capsule. He was dead from that moment. We were just starting to transfer the capsule to a cannister we'd brought with us when there was this bang. I remember the whole aircraft seemed to jump. All we could do was try and hang on. It happened so fast. After the bang I remember it got very hot. There was a bright light and then I was just lifted up. I was flying through the air. Then I must have blacked out . . . Simon must have been trapped in there . . . it was . . . '

'So we're no better off,' Duggan said.

'No, wait a minute.' Martin struggled to his feet and moved a little way towards the aircraft. 'The heat in there must have reached a pretty high temperature.'

'So?' asked Duggan.

The army doctor stepped forward. 'Heat kills bacteria,' he said. 'If the temperature inside that aircraft reached a high enough degree it may have been enough to penetrate the capsule and . . . '

'Burn the little buggers to a crisp?' Duggan suggested.

'A non-technical description,' Martin said, 'but accurate enough. If those bacteria play by the rules that is.'

'Meaning they might not have been destroyed?'

'Let me explain,' Martin said. 'We've had two extremes of temperature involved here. The very cold weather. Low temperature. Under normal circumstances low temperatures tend to retard the bacteria's ability to reproduce itself. To slow down the rate of infection. From what we've seen it doesn't appear to have affected the strain of bacteria in question. So if we go to the other end of the scale we might assume that it is resistant to heat as well. But that isn't necessarily so. This *is* an extremely unstable bacteria. Possibly it might be killed off by high temperature, even though it isn't bothered by low.'

'We aren't going to find out until that fire dies down,' Duggan said.

'And until then,' Martin pointed out, 'we can't afford to lift the isolation order. The situation stays the same, Sergeant.'

Martin began to walk towards the command helicopter. He needed to talk to Kevin Markfield. His body throbbed with pain. He knew he was very lucky to be alive. Though he didn't want to he found himself turning towards the aircraft. He stood and watched it for a minute, aware of how fragile the hold on life really was. It could be snapped in an instant. In a scant moment of horror. He had come so very close himself. The thought made him break out in a cold sweat. So very, very close.

*   *   *

The water was colder than Harrison Bryant could ever have imagined. Yet after a while it didn't seem to bother him so much. Perhaps it was because he had too much on his mind. Too much to occupy him.

For one thing he was trying to keep both himself and Jenny alive. In his own case it wasn't too bad — but for Jenny it had become critical. When the car had slithered into the river, taking them both with it, Harrison had found himself reluctant to break free from Jenny's grip. He could have done easily. A few quick strokes would have taken him back to the bank, and apart from a thorough soaking he would have been fine. But there was no way he could have done that to Jenny. Nothing would have induced him to abandon her to the cold, merciless depths of that river.

As the Triumph had rolled over on its side, sinking into the mud at the bottom of the river, they had both been completely submerged. Harrison had swallowed a mouthful of water, and he fought to raise his head above the surface. Panic had gripped him at first because he had no way of knowing how far down they'd gone. Then his head had broken clear and he had gulped in great breaths of cold air, coughing wildly and spitting water from his mouth. He could feel Jenny, still clinging to him, her slim body jerking beneath the surface. Bracing his feet against the submerged seat of the car he had grasped her under the arms and hauled her up. Her head came out of the water, eyes wide open, mouth sucking in air. Her dark hair was streaked across her face in glistening strands, plastered to the contours of her skull. Harrison raised her as high as he could before her trapped ankle stopped him. Jenny fumbled about under the water and caught hold of the edges of the doorframe to support herself. She was just able to keep her head clear of the water. The rest of her body remained submerged. They stayed still for a while. Letting the car settle. Allowing their racing emotions to calm down.

'Jenny, I think I'll have to go and fetch help,' Harrison said slowly.

The moment he spoke the words he realised it had been the wrong thing to say.

He saw the terror in her eyes. She was ready to go to pieces at the thought of him abandoning her. He knew then he couldn't leave her. Not even for a little while. He was her only hope.

'Hey!' he said. 'Easy, now. Let's forget I said that. I'm not going anywhere.' He reached out and stroked the dark hair away from her pale, cold, wet face. 'Don't worry, Jenny, I'm going to get you out of this!'

He made the words sound confident; inside he was desperately trying to come up with physical action to back them up.

$$\star \quad \star \quad \star$$

'Kemp!' Sergeant Wendover threw his protective suit's headgear across the command helicopter and slumped wearily on one of the hard, narrow seats. 'I should have known that little prick was just waiting for a chance! I knew it and I let it bloody happen!'

Martin glanced across the rim of his mug of hot tea. He couldn't help noticing the hard gleam that showed in Sergeant Duggan's eyes.

'Should *I* be interested in this?' Martin asked.

'One of my men has gone,' Wendover explained. 'Deserted. His rifle and suit are all we've found.'

'You seemed to imply his desertion was imminent.'

Wendover picked up a spare mug of tea. 'It's been on the cards for a good time.' He took a long swallow from the mug. 'Kemp should never have joined the army. He realised it soon after he got in, and all he wanted after that was to get out.'

'On the other hand . . . ' Martin said, ' . . . he may have left for another reason.'

Wendover frowned. 'You know something I don't?'

'Captain Mather managed to tell us something which might have a connection with this man Kemp's disappearance,' Martin said.

'He couldn't swear to it but he thinks he saw a second man just about the time he came into contact with the infected victim. The one who gave him the disease,' Duggan explained.

'This other man — the one the captain thinks he saw — could he be infected too?' Wendover's question was directed towards Martin.

'Until we know otherwise I have to assume he was.'

'Christ!' Wendover murmured. 'So where is he?'

Duggan said: 'We think he's got through our perimeter.'

'Another guess?'

'In the last half-hour we've tied up a couple of loose ends,' Martin said. 'First — a possible infected victim who seems to have vanished. Second — we do have a genuine missing person.'

'Positive or probable? Maybe he's buried somewhere under one of those wrecked buildings.'

Martin shook his head. 'No. He's alive — or he was. Inspector Henderson's search party found a badly injured young woman in one of the hotel rooms. Apparently she'd spent the weekend here in Shepthorne with her . . . boyfriend for want of a better word. He turns out to be a respectable city banker. Married with a family. When he realised what was going on he abandoned the girl. She was trapped in the wreckage of their room. The man — his name is Sam Mayhew — said he'd go for help. The girl knew he was running out on her. He must have expected her to die, so he took off in an attempt to keep his name out of any possible news reports.'

'Sounds a likeable chap,' Wendover said. 'So you think it's probable he might have picked up the infection?'

'That's how we have to treat it until we know for sure,' Martin said.

'And maybe this man came in contact with Kemp,' Duggan suggested. 'Could be why he ran.'

Wendover drained his mug. 'So what do we do?'

'Use the choppers,' Duggan said. 'Fly some search patterns over the area. See if we can spot either of them. A man on foot isn't going to get very far in this weather.'

'He isn't going to leave much in the way of a trail,' Wendover warned. 'Not while this damn snow keeps coming.'

'I appreciate the problems,' Martin said. 'But if we're right and these *are* infected carriers they mustn't be allowed to make further contacts.'

'What do we do if we locate them?' Wendover asked. 'Shoot them on sight?'

Martin fixed his gaze on the waiting sergeant. 'If you find them and confirm the infection — yes! They *must* be stopped! Shot and the bodies burned!'

'Are you coming with us?' Duggan asked.

'No. I can't leave here until I've confirmed the condition of the bacteria on that plane.'

A few minutes later Martin stood and watched two of the army helicopters lift off and rise into the falling mist of snow. The pulsing roar of the engines faded away, muffled by the drifting curtain of white.

2

Downing Street, London

'Yes, Kevin, I see.' The PM listened in silence to the voice on the other end of the line. 'I suppose we were expecting too much. There were too many factors beyond our control. All we can do now is to try and conclude this matter as expeditiously as possible. The most important consideration is the locating and destroying of these two unfortunate men if they *are* found to be carrying the bacteria. After that has been accomplished we can attempt to salvage some kind of political dignity from this terrible tragedy.'

* * *

Markfield put down the telephone. He glanced at the two other men in the office.

'I'd like you gentlemen to take a little ride with me,' he said.

Decker smiled. 'You mean we come whether we like it or not.'

'You still don't trust us, do you, Markfield?' Jerry Chapman asked.

'It's that kind of world.'

'Bloody rubbish,' Chapman said. 'You create suspicion because of the deception surrounding every word you utter. You twist fact and shatter faith. You use words as weapons and then you wonder why the world is in such a mess.'

'A necessary evil,' Markfield said. 'The word is as much your weapon as it is mine. Or are you going to tell me you never manipulate any of the information that comes into your hands?'

Decker got up from behind his desk. He took a worn sheepskin topcoat from a hook on the wall and pulled it on. 'In-depth arguments from you two I can do without today,' he said, and opened the office door.

A couple of Markfield's men stood in the corridor. They made no show of the fact but both were armed; and being

Markfield's men they were fully capable *and* prepared to use the weapons they carried if the need arose. Markfield had a quick word with them before he led Decker and Chapman to the lift which took them to the ground floor and from there to the outside of the building.

The station's car park was closed off by several carefully placed cars, and there were a number of men positioned around the building.

As Markfield stepped through the glass doors he heard the throb of an approaching helicopter. The machine materialised a couple of minutes later, dropping down out of the snow-laden sky. It swung in over the car park, then settled lightly, the whirling rotors tearing up clouds of powdery snow and hurling it across the open area in icy billows.

'Gentlemen!' Markfield said.

They clambered, gratefully, inside the helicopter, letting its cocoon of warmth surround them as it swept up from the car park and began the return journey to Shepthorne.

Sam Mayhew fell again. He lay with his face buried in cold, deep snow. It felt soothing against his burning, crawling flesh. Even his hands itched — and the sensation was beginning to spread across his whole body. He wouldn't look at his hands any more because the sight of them made him want to vomit. The raw, bleeding, open sores. The swollen joints and discoloured flesh. If he'd had anything left to bring up he would have done. But there was nothing left to evacuate from his tortured stomach. He had gone through the retching cycle earlier, his body bent double in agony, heaving violently until he'd coughed up dark streaks of blood. Now he was experiencing an overpowering weariness. A deep lassitude. It was why he kept falling down. His head ached too. Not a normal pain. This was an awesome, grinding ache that hammered across the top of his skull.

Sam was scared. He knew he was ill — but he had no way of knowing how ill, or what was wrong with him, let alone what had caused it. He'd lost count of the times he'd fallen and climbed to his feet again. He had long since given up trying to keep track of where he was going. If he'd been able to think clearly he would have realised he was lost. But it was unlikely that Sam Mayhew would ever think clearly again. With infinite slowness the bacteria now overwhelming his entire body was insidiously attacking the outer fringes of his brain, initiating the destruction of living cells. An irreversible process . . .

With a great deal of effort Sam pushed up off the ground. He knelt in the snow, head sagging forward on his chest.

I'm hurting — the small voice spoke clearly to him, rising out of the dark well of misery threatening to overwhelm him totally — *dear God, I'm hurting. In pain. My flesh rotting in front of my eyes. My skin crawling as if it was covered by a million scratching insects. What's happening to me? How did it happen? Why? And what can I do? Nowhere to go — no place to hide — no one to turn to . . .*

Some surviving inner strength forced him to his feet. Sam stood uncertainly, swaying gently. Twice he began to move and each time he drew back, peering about him with streaming eyes. He saw nothing. Only the thick blanket of snow on the ground and the shifting curtain of white that fell silently from a curve of pale sky.

He finally moved on, plodding with infinite slowness across a wide and seemingly endless plain of white.

★　★　★

Shivering violently, Larry Kemp pulled his jacket tighter around his body and drew himself deeper in the thick undergrowth. He hadn't realised how cold it was. He was beginning to wish he'd waited before taking off. Given himself a better chance. He should have been more prepared. Had extra clothing — civilian clothing — maybe some food or even . . . he swore angrily. No! He'd been right to do it! The longer he'd waited the worse things would have become. The more he thought about the day's operation in that village, the more sure he was that he *had* done the right thing. If he'd stayed he could easily have ended up dead like those other poor buggers! Even the bloody officers were affected. They were the ones who usually managed to stay healthy, no matter what the situation. But not this time. Not even Captain bloody Mather! No point in hanging around a place like Shepthorne. Larry, he smiled to himself, you did the right thing this time! You looked out for yourself. Well, nobody else would. Still, it wouldn't harm if he could get warm a bit. He didn't reckon this fuckin' weather. Enough to curl an Eskimo's toes.

He sat upright and stared out at the falling snow. Wouldn't be so bad if he knew where he bloody was! That was one thing he regretted now. His inattention during orientation instruction. If he'd listened to what they'd been trying to teach him then he would have been able to work out his position and plan a route. Kemp sighed. Too bloody late now, Larry boy, because you couldn't figure out where you are at this moment if you had the entire resources of the AA and RAC behind you!

He stumbled to his feet, knocking the clinging snow from his clothes. He pulled the collar of his jacket up as far as it would go. Casting around he finally made a choice and made off through the thick stand of trees. Maybe he'd find a road on the other side. Or even the motorway. He didn't care as long as he came across some form of human signs.

He pushed on, head down, hands thrust deeply in the pockets of his jacket. The snow clung to his face, matting his hair. It stung his eyes and got in his mouth each time he opened it to take a breath. Without warning he stepped in a pool of water concealed beneath a thick layer of snow. He splashed about angrily, feet sinking into the soft, sodden grass, desperately trying to locate firm ground. By the time he did his boots were full of water and his trousers wet up to the knees. There wasn't a thing he could do about it so he carried on. After a couple of minutes the water chilled his flesh and he felt the cold encase his feet.

Kemp staggered on. He had to keep pressing forward. There was no going back on the path he had chosen.

★　★　★

Martin made his way along the village street. He'd removed the protective suit. Thankfully he didn't need it any longer. His inspection of the capsule inside the plane had verified his earlier hopes. The bacteria *had* been destroyed in the fire. It solved one problem. It did nothing to help the even more deadly threat posed by the possibility of one — and maybe even two — infected people somewhere outside the village. The thought horrified him. The bacteria in action, even within the confines of the village, had illustrated its potency, the speed with which it could be transmitted from one person to another. Martin found himself picturing the mass epidemic that might be unleashed if the bacteria was introduced to some heavily populated area. He shuddered at the thought. And there was no effective cure for the damn disease yet.

Discovery that the bacteria on the plane had been destroyed had left Martin with a feeling of helplessness. The bacteria was needed so that tests could be carried out to develop the neutralising agent. Now there was no bacteria. Unless . . . It had taken a minute or so for the answer to sink in. He *did* still have live bacteria. In the bodies of the two infected people still in the village. Peter Mather and the woman Allison Smythe.

He had made contact with his research station by radio from the helicopter that had flown him in. Martin had explained the situation to the head of his research unit, and it had been agreed the only course open to them was to fly the victims to the research station. There they could be placed in isolation and used in an attempt to develop the neutralising agent.

Martin was met by Inspector Henderson and Vivian Dolby. Both men were filthy, their clothing stained and torn. Nearby, in a clear area, huddled in rescued blankets and coats, were the survivors of Shepthorne. Henderson and Dolby, aided by Mike Sandler and Henderson's sergeant, had painstakingly gone through the wrecked, gutted buildings, searching, listening, often digging with their bare hands to drag out some entombed but still living villager. They had found a lot of dead people. Shepthorne would find it had paid a high price for the folly of others.

'Well?' Henderson asked.

'The bacteria *has* been destroyed,' Martin told him.

Dolby gave a deep sigh. 'Thank God for that.'

'It isn't completely over yet,' Martin said.

'Haven't we been through enough?' Henderson snapped. 'What are you going to throw at us now?'

'I've arranged for Captain Mather and Allison Smythe to be flown out of here. They'll be taken to the research station I work at and with luck we may be able to develop the anti-bacteria agent we need.'

'Will you try to actually *cure* them if

the thought crosses your minds?' Henderson asked coldly.

Martin glanced at the policeman. 'I can understand your bitterness towards me, Inspector,' he said, 'but at least give me credit for trying to solve this problem.'

'Let me point out one thing, Doctor,' Henderson replied. 'In the first place none of this would have happened if there hadn't been research into germ-warfare. Without the research there wouldn't have been the need for the flight of that damned aircraft. There wouldn't have been any crash. This village would not have been destroyed. People would not have died. And we would not be in the position we are now. With two potential victims of your foul disease running free and liable to infect God knows how many more. Do you still want me to give you a pat on the back?'

Martin turned abruptly and walked away.

'I heard what you were saying to the Inspector,' Elouise Smythe said, falling in beside Martin. 'Do you think it might be possible to save my sister?'

'I honestly don't know,' Martin admitted. 'We're dealing with a completely new strain of bacteria. One that is virtually running wild. We need time to work on it. Only time is the one thing we haven't got.'

'You people are Allison's only chance.' Elouise glanced at her sister's blanket-wrapped form. 'I really don't understand what this is all about. But you will try and save her?'

'We'll do what we can,' Martin said. Which is very damn little! Because we don't know what we're dealing with!

★   ★   ★

'We haven't seen a bloody thing,' Duggan yelled into the mike. He hated using the radio during a flight. He adjusted the headset, trying to catch Sergeant Wendover's reply.

' . . . just have to keep widening the pattern.'

'I don't think we ought to go out too far. They can't have covered too much distance. Not in this weather. And not over this terrain.'

'Let's give it another try,' Wendover said.

* * *

Markfield stood and watched the helicopter containing Peter Mather and Allison Smythe lift off and vanish over a line of trees. He hunched his shoulders beneath his coat, turning to cast a calculated glance at the scene of desolation spread out before him.

'Must have been a pleasant little place,' he observed 'Someone is going to receive a hell of a bill for compensation when this mess is sorted out.'

'You could help towards that by allowing the emergency services in now,' Martin suggested. 'Face it, Markfield. The cat is out of the bag. Coming down with the heavy hand isn't necessary any more.'

'I'm acutely aware of that,' Markfield said testily. 'So much for me trying to keep it all quiet.'

'You tried. It didn't work, Markfield. Look, we were up against too many disadvantages. Even super-efficient logic sometimes fails to come up with the required effect. Hell, man, we were dealing with something that just got out of control. Maybe it's a lesson to learn. That we can be caught off guard as well as the next man.' Martin paused. 'Let's face it, this whole bloody affair has been one almighty cockup! I don't think any of us are going to come out of it smelling very sweet!'

There was a shout from the command helicopter. Martin and Kevin Markfield made their way across to it. The radio operator was waiting for them.

'I've just spoken to Sergeant Duggan. He thinks he's got one of them spotted.'

* * *

No sooner had he laid eyes on the narrow road edging the field he was crossing than the familiar sound of an approaching helicopter reached his ears.

Larry Kemp twisted round. Bloody hell! Of all the luck! Just as he'd found a road! He watched the dark shape of the helicopter loom in over the crest of a low rise behind him. It sank low, coming in no more than ten or twelve feet above the ground, trailing a stream of snow in its wake. The noise of the rotors increased.

He turned and ran on. Forgetting how cold he was. How tired from dragging himself, half-frozen across all those fields. Over fences and through thorny hedge-rows. He was wet and muddy and miserable. But he was still determined to get away from the army. If they wanted him back they were going to have to come and fetch him.

He couldn't believe it when he found he'd reached the low fence. An excited chuckle bubbled from the corners of his thin mouth as he scrambled over the fence. He lost his footing and fell, rolling down the steep, snowy bank to the road below. Picking himself up Kemp began to run along the road. He could hear the helicopter somewhere behind and above him. He threw a defiant glance up at the squat machine. It hovered overhead like some great brown bug. But it couldn't get to him because of the trees edging the narrow road.

Sod you! Bloody bastards! Can't leave a body alone. He ignored the insistent throb of the engines, not even bothering to look up when a second helicopter joined the first. The two machines drifted along with him, like a pair of anticipatory vultures.

Kemp felt a cold ache in his stomach. He stopped walking and eyed the road ahead. The trees and thick hedges vanished up ahead. From a point no more than twenty-five yards further on the ground levelled out. Only flat grass verges edged the road.

Kemp moved to the side of the road and peered through a section of hedge. A frown creased his pale face. Beyond the hedge lay an empty field. On the far side lay a deep wood. Tall trees rose in thick ranks that climbed a long slope. He studied the field. If he could get across there and into the wood he'd stand a better chance than if he stayed on the road. It was going to be a long run across that field. But it had to be attempted.

He wriggled through the hedge, gasping and swearing as sharp thorns pierced his clothes and scratched his flesh. One hooked itself in the soft flesh of his left cheek, tearing a nasty gash that began to bleed. Then he was through, scrambling to his feet. He didn't wait to check on how close the helicopters were. Simply dug in his heels and began to run.

Across the field.

Towards the line of dark trees that seemed a long way away.

It was hard going. Beneath the snow lay mud that clung to his boots. Slowed him down. Made his legs ache each time he raised a foot. Come on! Come on! Don't let the bastards beat you now! You can make it. He stared at the trees ahead of him. They didn't seem to be getting any closer. That was imagination. They *had* to be getting closer. His chest started to burn. Breath snatched in his throat. Sweat coated his face and turned icy cold. He stumbled. Kicked angrily at the gluey mud that clung to his boots in fat lumps.

Over his shoulder came a black shadow. Racing ahead of him. Stark against the white snow. The air throbbed to the beat of the helicopter's motors. The thwack-thwack-thwack of the great rotors dinned in his ears. He could feel the power of the driven wind bearing down on him. Off to one side, out of the corner of one eye, he caught a glimpse of the second helicopter. It was coming to rest. Almost before it touched the ground he saw the door slide open.

A uniformed figure jumped out, crouching as the heavy boots sank in the snow.

There was something familiar about the man. Kemp turned his head fully, and a shrill protest burst from his lips.

Sergeant Wendover!

He should have known that son of a bitch would come after him. Of all the bastards in the army he had to get Wendover.

Well you haven't got me yet! He glanced towards the trees. A wild grin split his face. He was almost there. Not far now. If he could get into the shadowed darkness of that wood . . .

Go to hell, Wendover! Take your rotten, sodding army and stuff it right up your arse!

'Kemp!'

He heard the strident bellow even over the heavy sound of the helicopters.

'Kemp!'

He didn't even look around. Why should he when victory was in his grasp! He was free and almost clear! Only a few more yards to . . .

He didn't hear the first shot. Only the second. Even that was as a faint, distant sound. Because by then he was already falling, his body screaming in silent agony as the two bullets ripped into, through, and out of him. They did enough physical damage to his vital organs to ensure certain death. By the time he hit the ground, numbed, helpless, blood already spurting from the pulpy wounds in his flesh, his mind was closing out reality. His mouth was wide open, but no sound came from it. His eyes were open, though he saw very little. He struck the ground and slithered in an ungraceful arc, leaving behind a trail of blood to dapple the churned snow. He rolled and bounced and twisted over and over, finally coming to rest on his back, one arm twisted under him, legs splayed wide apart. His body twitched, one leg flicking against the ground. Blood pulsed thickly from the glistening cavity in his left side. Splintered ribs gleamed white. He didn't see, or hear, the approaching figures. He was dying, and in his last moments of rational thought, he wondered why. It was wrong — it had to be wrong — they didn't kill people just because they deserted . . . and he died still wondering why it had happened.

'I don't see any signs of the infection,' Duggan said, bending over the body.

'Maybe I should have asked him,' Wendover remarked. He was unmoved by the incident. He swung his rifle over one shoulder. 'We couldn't take the chance, Andy. Come on. There's still another one to find.'

Duggan backed away from the body. He unstrapped a can of fuel from the side of the helicopter. Returning to the body he doused it with the fuel. Stepping back he lit a match and tossed it on to the body. There was a soft thump and the fuel ignited. Duggan turned away as the flames began to blister Kemp's white face. The stench of burning flesh and hair lodged in his nostrils before he moved away. He replaced the can of fuel and climbed back inside the helicopter. As it lifted off, to follow Wendover's machine, the draught from the rotors fanned the flames consuming Kemp's body.

Duggan couldn't help but wonder. Had Kemp been infected? Or had he been nothing more than a scared kid doing what a hell of a lot of scared kids had done before and would do again! Duggan found he suddenly needed to know the answer — he also knew it was unlikely he ever would.

★　★　★

There was no way at first to bring in vehicles, so the emergency services were obliged to manhandle their equipment. A number of uniformed police arrived first, followed by ambulance crews and a couple of doctors. They set about their tasks with controlled efficiency, forgetting the frustrations of the past hours, and concentrating on attending to the injured.

Kevin Markfield watched the activity with total indifference. His mind was on other things. He could see one hell of a row brewing over this shambles. What was it the PM had said? Something about salvaging a degree of political dignity from the affair. Markfield allowed himself a thin smile. It wasn't political dignity requiring salvation — more like political survival. Once the news of this broke — and despite all his efforts it *would* eventually break now — the bang would be heard all the way to Washington and back. The Americans would get their share of tar and feathers. Somewhere blame would be laid. And some poor sacrificial lambs would be led into the sunlight and executed for all the world to see. There would be a great shaking of heads and a seemingly endless flow of hypocritical breast-beating. Fingers would point, threats would be made, and after the dust had died down it would all begin again.

'Sergeant Wendover to speak to you, Mr Markfield.'

Markfield leaned inside the helicopter and told the radio operator to switch to the internal speaker. There was a soft hum of static.

'Markfield here.'

'Wendover. One down — one to go!'

'Don't take too long. It's going to be dark in an hour.'

★   ★   ★

Elouise Smythe watched as two ambulance men lifted the stretcher holding Dawn Stanton and began to carry her along the road.

'Will she live?' she asked the young doctor who had attended to Dawn.

'After what she's been through I wouldn't like to hazard a guess. Apart from her injuries she's suffering from exposure and the loss of a great deal of blood. If we'd been able to get to her sooner things might not be so critical. The same applies to a lot of the people I've looked at. Just what has been going on here?'

Elouise smiled. 'To be honest, Doctor,

I'm not entirely sure myself.'

The doctor moved on, leaving Elouise alone for a while. She pulled her coat around her, shivering slightly. Her thoughts returned to Allison. Somehow she knew she wouldn't see her sister again — not alive at least.

'Are you all right, my dear?'

Vivian Dolby took her hand and led her along the street. Neither of them looked back.

'Where are we going?' Elouise asked.

'I've been speaking to one of the police officers. Apparently they have arranged temporary accommodation for anyone who needs it. At a guest house in Luscombe. If we make our way along the road a car will take us there.'

'What do we do then?'

Dolby smiled. 'Why, Elouise, my dear, we carry on. We simply live.'

★ ★ ★

'The woman was dead on arrival, Martin. The man died ten minutes ago.'

Martin stared at the radio speaker. 'Did

you manage to isolate any of the bacteria?'

'Yes.'

'Is it enough?'

'We'll make it enough.'

'I'll speak to you later.'

★　★　★

'Are you certain you saw him?'

Duggan nodded. 'I saw him. He's in there.'

Wendover took a long look at the big, stonebuilt barn. He checked his rifle before glancing at Duggan.

'Ready?'

They walked across the uneven ground, the wind driving the cold snow at their backs. In front of them the huge old building loomed darkly skywards. When they reached the front of the barn they were able to see where one of the big doors had been pulled open, dislodging the snow that had formed a small drift.

Duggan edged inside. He moved to the left, sensing Wendover's entry off to the right. The two soldiers stood motionless, letting their eyes adjust to the gloom. Solid shapes began to form out of the greyness.

The floor of the barn was littered with old pieces of abandoned farm machinery, gathered piles of odds and ends long since forgotten. At the far end of the barn a narrow flight of sagging wooden steps ran up the wall to a hayloft. Thin shafts of light speared down from holes in the high roof.

Moving away from the door Duggan worked his way across the dirty floor. He saw something glistening just ahead of him. Duggan crouched. It was blood. Thick and dark, streaked with some pale yellow fluid. Duggan ran his gaze along the floor of the barn. There were more of the blood spots — an uneven trail of them leading towards the far end of the building.

Duggan's hands were clammy with sweat. He wiped each one in turn on his pants. Damn this bloody pantomime! He cast his eyes back and forth across the barn. Come on, he begged, show yourself! He couldn't wait to get out of this place.

Back into the open air. Out of this dusty old wreck. It even smelled of death . . .

Wendover's warning yell came a fraction too late. If Duggan hadn't allowed his mind to drift — even for that fraction of a second — he might have noticed the dark shape detach itself from the dense shadow around a rusting tractor.

Realising he was already too late, Duggan attempted an evasive manoeuvre. It was futile. He felt the heavy bulk strike him, knock him off balance. Then the figure was bending over him, breath coming from it in snuffling gasps. A sickening stench filled Duggan's nostrils and clutched at his throat. His stomach rebelled and he only just kept himself from retching. He tried to scramble away from the lurching figure but it moved with him. The terrible smell increased — the smell of decay and sickness — the all pervading stench of rotting flesh.

And in a brief instant the dark figure stepped into a shaft of light coming down from the high roof. Duggan saw but found it hard to believe what he was looking at. This thing. This obscene, grotesque object surely could never have been a man.

There was no face left to speak of. Just a featureless mask of swollen flesh and running sores. The eyes were lost in protruding rolls of dark, puffy flesh. Cheeks were distorted, burst blisters oozing a sticky pus. A red gash indicated the mouth. It sagged loosely open, revealing a thick, swollen tongue. The clothing had been ripped and shredded, exposing flesh overrun with bulging swellings, wet, sticky sores that penetrated deep into the body. The hands reaching out towards Duggan were swollen out of all proportion, the thick fingers dark-fleshed, streaked with blood from scratching violently at the irritating sores.

The thing that had once been Sam Mayhew emitted a low moan. He took a faltering step forward, reaching out to close his swollen and bloody hands over Duggan's face. Duggan let out a scream of revulsion as the hands clutched at his flesh. He kicked back, desperate to get away from the infected man.

Sam Mayhew refused to let him go.

Even as Duggan struggled to free himself from the grip of the infected hands clamped around his face, Wendover — choosing his moment — lifted his rifle and pumped half a dozen bullets into Sam Mayhew's body. The impact of the bullets slammed Sam back across the barn. He backpeddled wildly, trying to stay on his feet. Blood and flesh and bone filled the air around him as the bullets chewed their way through his bacteria-ravaged body. As Sam smashed heavily to the floor, writhing in bloody agony, Wendover stepped up close, aimed quickly, and emptied the rest of the rifle's magazine at Sam's head. The range was close, no more than a couple of feet. The high-velocity bullets ripped Sam's head apart, spilling a gory splash of blood and brains across the barn floor. Sam kicked a few times and then lay still.

Wendover turned from the bleeding corpse. He ejected the empty magazine and clicked in a fresh one. He glanced across to where Duggan was crouched, frantically scrubbing at the sides of his face with his hands. Wendover didn't speak. He walked carefully round behind Duggan, stared at the back of his friend's head for a moment, then put two bullets through Duggan's skull. Duggan half rose to his feet, his arms swinging wide of his body. A bright stream of blood jetted out from one of the bullet holes in his skull. A thicker spurt burst from the exit holes made by the two bullets. Duggan pitched face down in the dirt. His left hand scrabbled at the floor, fingers drumming fiercely. Then a long tremor made his body arch, then relax. The steady jet of blood slackened, died, ceased. It was as easy as that to end a man's life.

Pushing open the barn door Wendover stepped outside, breathing in the cold air. He crossed to the closest helicopter, tossed his rifle inside the machine, and then unstrapped the can of fuel. He returned to the barn. Opening the can he doused both bodies well, then spread the remaining fuel across the floor.

He stood in the open doorway and took a lighter from his pocket. Lighting it he crouched and touched the flame to the wet trail of fuel. The dancing flame shot along the floor, reaching the bodies. Wendover stood and stared at Duggan's body, watching it become encased in a burst of flame. Then he shook his head, almost as if he was awakening from a deep sleep, turned and walked outside.

He returned to the waiting helicopters, signalling the pilots to prepare for liftoff. He climbed into his machine, closing the door as the helicopter lifted off the ground.

He hadn't even noticed that the snowfall was slackening off.

Below the ascending helicopters the old barn blazed with boiling flame and thick coils of smoke that rose into the cold sky.

The helicopters drifted away. Silence returned, broken only by the subdued roar of the flames consuming the barn. The roof caved in with a rush of flame, red embers and sparks exploding briefly. Sooty ashes drifted out across the field, streaking the white snow with dirty smudges . . .

★   ★   ★

Jenny couldn't stop her teeth from chattering. The cold had penetrated deeply now and her whole body was reacting to the low temperature. She was having difficulty in keeping her head above water. It was taking all of her concentration and will-power to maintain her grip on the doorframe; if she had relaxed for an instant she knew there would be no chance of retaining her hold. She would have slipped below the water and it would all have been over.

There was a rush of air bubbles rising to the surface. Seconds later Harrison's head appeared. He sucked in deep breaths of air, shaking his head to clear his eyes of water.

'This time, Jenny,' he said. 'No fooling. I'll stay down there until I do it.'

She made to reply, but he simply grinned, and disappeared from sight. She stared at the spot, watching the ripples roll away and vanish. She knew that he must be as weary as she was. Countless times he'd pulled himself beneath the water, struggling in the darkness to free her trapped ankle. Jenny couldn't even feel what he was doing any more. All she could do was to hang on, and wait, and hope that the car didn't settle any deeper.

The Triumph moved at that precise moment. Jenny felt it tremble and then begin to tilt over. She tried to lean in the opposite direction, aware that if the car kept on settling it would eventually roll on its roof. And that would mean her whole body being pulled beneath the surface of the water.

'No!' she moaned; more in anger than despair. 'Not now . . . not after all this time!'

There was a rapid surge of huge bubbles breaking the surface of the water. Again the car moved. Jenny, in desperation, reached out towards the bank. It was too far away. She remained in that position, her left arm stretched out, fingers stiff, and her hand was the last part of her to slide beneath the surface of the water as the Triumph completed its roll and settled on the river bed. The dark water frothed, bubbles bursting in a muddy swirl . . .

'You found him?' Martin asked.

Wendover's voice crackled through the speaker.

'And dealt with him . . . '

Martin breathed a sigh of relief. 'Are you on your way back?'

'I am,' Wendover replied shortly.

Martin frowned at his tone. He glanced at Markfield who shrugged. 'Is something wrong?'

'Andy Duggan's dead. He came into contact with Mayhew. I had no choice, did I, Doctor? I had to shoot him and burn *him* as well.'

'I'm sorry.'

'Are you? Not as sorry as I am. Andy Duggan and I were old mates. We went back a long way. He'd better not have died for nothing.'

Martin stared at the speaker. He was at a loss for words. What the hell could he say? He heard the sound of the contact being broken.

'It appears to be over,' Markfield said. He eased off his seat and moved to the door of the command helicopter.

Martin looked out through the door and gazed at the scattered groups of people moving back and forth along the street of the ruined village. 'It isn't going to be over for those poor devils for a long time. Or don't they come under your department's responsibility, Markfield?'

Markfield glanced over his shoulder as he prepared to climb out of the helicopter. 'Actually they don't,' he said, almost cheerfully. Then he said: 'The snow seems to be easing off!'

Martin stared at his back as Markfield strode off along the street. 'Bastard!' he muttered forcibly.

The corporal in charge of the radio glanced up. 'Sir?'

Martin shook his head. 'Nothing. Just thinking out loud.' Then he got up. Regardless of what Markfield thought, it wasn't over yet for some.

★ ★ ★

Decker, Chapman and Mike Sandler stood together, watching the activity around them. They didn't speak. All that they saw and all that they heard was filed away. Stored for future use. Somehow, some way, this story had to be told. It had escalated far beyond its original premise. The security blackout had failed. The hope of containing the bacteria had also failed, though the consequences had not been as horrendous as they might have been. Even so there had been a number of deaths that were going to be difficult to explain away.

The more Decker thought about it the angrier he became. Too many people had died here today. A community had been practically wiped out of existence. And for what? Would any real, lasting benefit come from all the misery and horror and suffering? He doubted it. And he knew that he couldn't let it rest . . . wouldn't . . . it would mean a fight . . . all the way down the line . . . but Decker had always maintained that the only good story was the one that *was* worth fighting for.

★ ★ ★

233

'I think that's our car,' Vivian Dolby said. He guided Elouise through the gathering crowd of reporters and TV cameramen towards the waiting vehicle. He felt her hesitate, hold back. 'Look straight ahead. Don't say a word, and don't stop until we reach that car.'

It was only as Elouise sank into the soft rear seat and the car moved off that she did speak.

'You see I won't know what to do on my own!'

Dolby glanced at her. He had known her for a number of years, as a neighbour and as a business woman, and had always been impressed by her ability to cope. Her clearheaded, logical approach to the problems of everyday life. Now he was seeing her in a new light. She was suddenly vulnerable. Liable to be easily hurt now that the removal of her responsibility for the shop and her sister had created a vacuum. While the shop had been there, and Allison, Elouise's life had been too full to allow her time for reflection; the tragic events of the day had wiped away her world and now Elouise was able to stand back and consider her future. Dolby knew the feeling — it was the way he himself had been feeling only a few hours earlier.

'Perhaps there won't be a need for you to be on your own,' he said gently.

Elouise stared at him for such a long time that Dolby found himself becoming distinctly uncomfortable. And then she reached out to lay her hands over his. A hint of tears moistened her eyes.

'Oh, Major . . . thank you.'

⋆　⋆　⋆

An occasional bubble rose to the dark surface of the water. For an instant it remained — a transparent, fragile thing destined to exist for no longer than a few brief seconds . . .

The expanding ripples had barely faded before a sudden and violent eruption below the surface threw up a silver stream of bubbles. Displaced water swirled in dark eddies. It geysered upwards as a thrashing shape burst clear.

Sucking precious air into her aching,

starved lungs, Jenny Morrish fought to stay afloat. Her wide-eyed stare mirrored the terror she was reliving in her mind; the numbing horror of that seemingly endless submersion in the black depths; lungs straining for air that was denied them; her silent, frantic, weakening struggles — and then, almost too late, she became aware of herself rising. The realisation came to her slowly — she was free! Her trapped ankle had been freed! Jenny kicked wildly, arms thrusting against the water that no longer held her captive.

Twisting her head back and forth Jenny searched for Harrison. A coldness far more potent than the icy water engulfed her. She experienced a jolting sickness in her stomach as fear and dismay and shock combined to assault her already ravaged system. Please let him be alive! He must be! Don't let anything happen to him now that *I'm* all right!

She heard water splash behind her. As she twisted round, Harrison's white, but grinning face bobbed before her eyes.

' . . . I thought . . . ' she began.

He swam to her and guided her to the bank. Dragging himself out of the water he caught hold of her clothing and hauled her ungraciously on to the snow-covered grass beside him.

'I began to think I'd never get out,' she said. She began to shiver and huddled closer to him.

'There was no worry on that score,' Harrison said. He stroked wet strands of hair away from her cold white face.

'How could you be so sure?' she asked.

She failed to see the slight smile edging his mouth. 'After what you promised I just couldn't fail.'

'Oh? What was that?'

'An offer to let me have the night *before* the morning after! Or are you one of those girls who'll promise everything without delivering?'

It was Jenny's turn to smile. 'You'll never find out if we just sit here, Harrison Bryant.'

'I do believe you're right, Jenny Morrish.' He climbed stiffly to his feet, and reached down to help her up. 'Let's get out of here.'

★ ★ ★

Inspector Henderson faced Kevin Mark-field across a few feet of dirty, trampled snow. The antagonism between the two men had almost manifested itself in physical form.

'I'll have the military personnel removed as soon as I can,' Markfield said. 'There will have to be a guard on the plane though. Only until all the interested agencies and departments have concluded their investigations. And of course Doctor Cooper will remain and check that no bacteria remains active, or that there are any further infections. We doubt that eventuality. If anyone else had been infected it would have shown by now.'

'You may have more people to satisfy than you anticipate,' Henderson informed him. Markfield's eyebrows lifted a fraction. 'For a start the Chief Constable of the county is on his way. Should be here in a while. Let me tell you, Markfield, the Chief Constable is a bastard, and you won't scare him one little bit. It seems he's hopping mad over the way you've interfered with the police during this emergency. After him there are the heads of the local county councils. County Fire Chief. Area health authority. County Coroner. The general impression I got was that they are all somewhat upset at the way you've handled this matter, and frankly, Markfield, I can see their reasoning.'

Markfield sighed. Bloody officialdom! He turned away from Henderson and walked along the street. On an impulse he directed his steps towards the slope that angled down to the level of the river. For a moment he was out of sight of the village. Briefly alone. He stood and watched the dark flow of the water. At least the river looked peaceful. Undisturbed. He would have liked to have stayed there longer but he had too much to do. Contact the PM. Have a word with Thompson, the American liaison man — the son of a bitch must have had a premonition about what was going to happen and that was why he'd refused Markfield's invitation to sit in on the operation. Instead Thompson had stayed in the comfort of his London office.

Markfield turned and made his way up to the cluttered street, and back to the responsibilities of his profession.

If he'd stayed a minute longer he would have noticed the two figures huddled together on the edge of the riverbank. A young woman with dark hair and a tall man, his blond hair plastered to his skull. Both the woman and the man were soaked to the skin, and when they stood up to start walking slowly in the direction of the village, the man had to support the young woman. She was limping painfully, her left ankle badly swollen. Yet despite the cold, and the scene of total devastation, the young couple appeared to be deep in conversation — almost as if they were taking a casual stroll along some idyllic country lane on a warm summer's day . . .

* * *

The daylight slowly faded, and perversely, the temperature began to rise slightly. The daylong wind and the accompanying snowfall slackened. Emergency services personnel turned their faces skyward and anticipated a lessening of the harsh conditions, which could only help their efforts.

As darkness fell, and before the emergency services could erect and put into operation the powerful floodlights they were going to need during the long night ahead, a brief period of peace seemed to cloak Shepthorne. The fallen snow lying over the scene of destruction somehow eliminated the harsh, angular lines and brought a surrealistic beauty to the stricken village.

Even the burned-out Hercules — the catalyst in the deadly chain of events — adopted a gentler aspect, its bulky lines softened and rounded by the shroud of white.

Downing Street, London

The PM was speaking to the President of the United States.

' . . . and of course this is going to

mean a reassessment of our bacteriological programme. We must be prepared for the Soviets to get news of this near-disaster. However, we may be able to use it as a way of showing them we mean business. That we *are* serious about the total commitment we have made towards building up our capability in this area. That we mean to match them in every aspect of germ and chemical warfare. Don't you agree, Mr President . . . '

THE END

DEATH NEVER STRIKES TWICE

John Glasby

Suspecting his wife Janine of having an affair, businessman Charles Jensen hires private eye Johnny Merak to follow her. Merak learns that Jensen had divorced his first wife Arlene — who has since disappeared . . . Convinced that Jensen had arranged Arlene's murder, Arlene's sister, Barbara Winton, also approaches Merak to investigate. Ignoring warnings to drop his investigations, he's knocked unconscious, and wakes next to a woman's corpse — a woman who has been shot with his gun. Then the police arrive . . .

THE CROOKED STRAIGHT

Ernest Dudley

A mysterious series of factory and warehouse fires was creating havoc, and the police did not appear to be getting on the track. So the *Globe* newspaper hired private eye Nat Craig to see what he could discover. Craig's investigations lead him to suspect arson as part of an insurance fraud, but when two young women are found brutally murdered he soon realises that the arson and murders may be connected. But who is the mastermind behind it all?

THE OSHAWA PROJECT

Frederick Nolan

1945: the War is over. A secret meeting takes place in Oshawa, Ontario between two powerful players in the post-war US Army, Donald Rogers and Mike Rafferty. The fragile alliance between the USA and the Soviets is being threatened by the aggressive outspokenness of one man — Brigadier General George Campion. Rogers enlists Rafferty into plotting Campion's expert assassination, to be funded by the German Reichsbank's abandoned gold reserves. Rafferty accepts reluctantly. But even a war hero can outlive his usefulness . . .

ANCIENT SINS

Robert Charles

When a fifty-year-old human skull was discovered in a lorry-load of sugar beet, it came at an inconvenient time. Breckland CID was fully involved in a three-county police operation, with the targets for Operation Longship in their sights. However, the old wartime mystery could not be ignored. DS Judy Kane was assigned to unravel a tangled skein of ancient sins — but a tortuous trail of lost loves and fiery passions would lead her into terrible danger.

THE ARDAGH EMERALDS

John Hall

England in the 1890s. The world of Victoria and the Empire. This is the world, too, of AJ Raffles, man about town, who, assisted by his inept assistant Bunny Manders, is a successful jewel thief. The eight stories in this book recapture the spirit of the Naughty Nineties, when the gentleman burglar would put out his Sullivan cigarette, don a black mask, outwit a villain, and save a lady in distress — and all before going out to dinner!